RITUAL

Uttaran Das Gupta is a New Delhi-based writer and journalist. He writes columns on films and literature, and his first book of poems, *Visceral Metropolis*, was published in 2017. This is his first novel.

RITUAL

Uttaran Das Gupta

PAN

First published 2020 by Pan
an imprint of Pan Macmillan Publishing India Private Limited,
707, Kailash Building
26 K. G. Marg, New Delhi – 110 001
www.panmacmillan.co.in

Pan Macmillan, 6 Briset St, Farringdon, London EC1M 5NR
Associated companies throughout the world
www.panmacmillan.com

ISBN 978-93-89109-04-7

This is a work of fiction. All characters, locations and events are fictitious. Any resemblance to actual events or locales or persons, living or dead, is entirely coincidental.

1 3 5 7 9 8 6 4 2

Typeset in Joanna MT Std by Manmohan Kumar
Printed and bound in India by
Replika Press Pvt. Ltd.

For *Baba* (1952–2017)

Every time I return to Calcutta I feel it must be surely impossible that it can continue much longer like this…

…Yet it always does.

An interval of a year makes the visual impact more painful, the squalor more squalid, the poverty more militant, the despair more desperate…

…I find Calcutta an intimidating and even infernal city, unredeemed and probably doomed.

– Mrinal Sen

Padatik (1973)

PROLOGUE

Calcutta, 1 May 1984: The hoodless jeep that had been following the black-and-yellow Ambassador taxi since Howrah, overtook it right in the middle of Dhakuria Bridge. It stopped suddenly, blocking the road. Taxi driver Ramneek Singh rammed his feet on the brakes, hoping fervently that they would not malfunction as they sometimes did. The old car shuddered with the sudden change in inertia, every rusty screw protesting, tyres burning their imprint on the road, but finally screeched to a halt within a few feet. The passengers were jerked forward violently and the man sitting beside the driver bumped into the dashboard, knocking over a small, cheap digital clock. For some inexplicable reason, Ramneek's first instinct was to pick up the clock and set it straight. It was still working. The screen displayed the time as 2.13 p.m.

The very next instant, an iron rod landed on the windscreen, shattering it into a thousand pieces, raining shards of glass on Ramneek and the passenger beside him.

A group of six or ten men stepped out of the jeep, armed with iron rods, hockey sticks or bicycle chains, the lower half of their faces covered with handkerchiefs or towels. Within minutes, they had broken all the windows of the taxi. Pulling open the doors, they dragged out the passengers – three monks and a nun of a small religious sect that had become wildly popular over the past few years. The name of the sect was Vasant Sena, Ramneek remembered.

One of the attackers held Ramneek by the collar, slapped him around, broke his nose and punched him in the stomach. The taxi driver fell on his face. His assailant placed a foot on his head and parked a hockey stick right next to his nose. The hot surface of the road was burning the side of Ramneek's face and he knew he should have closed his eyes, but the scene unfolding in front of him was mesmerising, and he bore unwilling witness.

The bridge shook at frequent intervals because of the local trains passing underneath. By now a small crowd had gathered at the spot, but no one intervened. There was little resistance from the victims either. One of the monks tried to make a run for it but was promptly caught, and his legs broken. All three monks and the nun finally succumbed to the vicious assault, lost consciousness and collapsed on the road. One of the attackers took out a tin can of kerosene and doused the victims. Then, he set them on fire.

Three of the bodies were lifeless, unmoving, but one monk, engulfed in flames, got up, arms flailing wildly, ran to the edge of the bridge and jumped off.

Ramneek would always remember this moment: when the blaring horn of the train passing below and the cries of the falling man combined into a piercing crescendo, tearing through the hot summer afternoon.

PART ONE

ONE

The body of the first girl turned up on a vacant plot at Hindustan Park on 9 January 1989. The municipal corporation employee responsible for switching on the streetlamps was late that evening. A group of boys was playing cricket in the gathering darkness of dusk. The batsman hit an elevated shot and the green tennis ball ballooned over the derelict wall surrounding the plot. An old Art Deco building had stood there not very long ago. But after the current owner moved to New Jersey, developers, who bought the property, tore it down to construct a new block of flats. The new construction had not begun yet, and the plot was strewn with concrete debris and weed entangled with refuse. The hapless fielder who had the task of retrieving the lost ball climbed over the wall and was unenthusiastically kicking around broken bottles of beer when he came upon the body. He ran back to his friends, who alerted their parents, and one of them called the police.

By the time a sub-inspector and a constable from the Gariahat police station arrived on a loud Enfield motorcycle, the streetlamps had been lit. A small crowd, comprising the amateur cricketers and a few adults, had gathered at the spot and were conducting a conversation in agitated whispers. The sub-inspector recognized the local municipal councillor, a member of the Party, among them. Instead of approaching the crowd, he enquired in a loud voice where the body was. A few hands immediately pointed towards the vacant plot. Taking his service revolver out of its holster, the sub-inspector climbed over the derelict wall, indicating to the constable to follow him.

Later, after the team from the forensic department had scanned the area, collecting whatever they needed and taking pictures of the body, the sub-inspector had a chat with the boy who had discovered it, his parents and the local councillor. They all told him that they did not know the girl; she was not from the area. The councillor made a few statements about the deteriorating performance of the police department, and how he intended to raise the matter with the politburo and also write to the commissioner. The sub-inspector shrugged and lit a cigarette. The crowd had already started thinning away, going home to watch popular Hindi film songs on *Chitrahaar* or catch the evening news on their black-and-white TVs. An ambulance arrived to take away the body, blaring its horn uselessly, rudely punctuating the Rabindrasangeet emanating from a music school nearby.

The autopsy was performed well after midnight at the Katapukur morgue. The sub-inspector was sitting on an iron bench in the corridor outside the operating theatre, smoking one cigarette after another to stay warm. He was almost certain that like most cases of bodies of young girls being discovered, it was rape. The girl was around twelve or thirteen, maybe a little younger.

The doctor, however, said it wasn't rape.

'No?' The sub-inspector was very surprised. 'So what is it?'

The doctor looked down at the dirty floor of the corridor in which they were standing, shifting his weight from one foot to the other. The sub-inspector thought the uneasiness was unbecoming in a man who performed autopsies every night.

'Well?'

'There's something else,' said the doctor.

'What?'

In a low voice, the doctor replied: 'Her heart is missing.'

This made no sense to the sub-inspector, so he asked the doctor to explain.

'Someone has cut out the heart from her chest,' said the doctor.

The sub-inspector suddenly felt that the night had grown colder. He was about to ask the doctor for more details but was cut short as they heard the night duty compounder sealing the body into a freezer with a loud clang.

The body of Anasuya Chatterjee, twelve, a student of Welland Gouldsmith School, was found by a municipal worker, whose duties involved driving around a truck at dawn, sprinkling the streets with water. After completing a few rounds on the morning of 8 February 1989, he parked his truck near the gates of the Eastern Command cantonment on Gurusaday Dutta Road and was having tea and butter-toast at a roadside stall, when he saw a pack of feral dogs fighting crows at a garbage dump nearby.

He would later recall that he immediately knew something was wrong. So, he took out the iron rod he always kept in the truck, and ran towards the dump, shouting and waving the weapon above his head. Seeing him, the animals fled, but they didn't go too far. Regrouping at a short distance, they kept a watch on the human who had interrupted their breakfast.

It did not take the municipal worker long to figure out what had attracted the birds and the beasts. He had initially feared it was an infant, abandoned for being illegitimate – not an uncommon occurrence. But, what he saw was the naked body of a young girl, half-wrapped in a black polythene sheet. A daring crow had returned, and perching on the dead girl's forehead, was plucking out her left eye with sharp jabs of its beak.

He felt his insides churn violently as he bent over on the side of the road and threw up.

The police had no difficulty in identifying the body. Anasuya's parents had reported her missing a week ago after she failed to return home from school one afternoon. Her father was a senior marketing executive at the head office of a tea company that had gardens in Darjeeling and Assam; the mother was a schoolteacher. The hapless yet surprisingly stoic parents identified the body at the Katapukur morgue, where they had been summoned by the officer-in-charge of the Ballygunge police station. The officer noted how the grieving parents displayed little emotion. The father filled in all the forms with a steady hand, and they drove away in their white Padmini, following the small truck that was carrying the hearse.

As there was no ransom call, the police had initially presumed it to be a sex crime. The autopsy report, which came a week later, however, debunked this theory: Anasuya had not been raped. It also provided another piece of information which made the investigating officer very uneasy: the heart had been surgically removed from the body. The officer immediately arrived at the conclusion that the crime had been committed by illicit organ traders and noted his observations in the FIR.

The identity of the first girl was never determined. No one had reported her missing or had come to look for her. Maybe she was the daughter of migrant workers from Bihar or Bangladesh passing through the state; perhaps her parents or family had moved on when they thought they would never find her. The sub-inspector who had begun the investigation at first thought the anonymity pointed to an honour killing, which, though uncommon in the city, was not unheard of. But he couldn't reconcile this theory to the fact of the missing heart. You might hate your daughter for eloping with someone of a different religion or caste, for smearing the honour of your family, but would you cut her heart out? Frustrated by the lack of progress and reassured by the lack of interest in the case, either from his seniors or anyone else, the sub-inspector let the file sink to the bottom of the ever-increasing tower of papers on his desk. There was no lack of cases – theft, burglary, molestation. Ones that could actually be solved, and some even had the additional satisfaction of a monetary gain. Even if he managed to find out who the girl was and why she had been killed and who had killed her, it wouldn't really help advance his career, would it? A few weeks later, he was transferred to another police station, and after handing over the pending cases to his successor, he promptly forgot all about them.

It was not yet dawn when Bishu Mondal, armed with a red plastic bucket half-filled with water, arrived at the edge of the pond, not too far from the Tiljala slum where he lived with his wife and children. He was not in the habit of coming here every morning to do his business. In fact, he had suffered from acute constipation since 1971, when he and his elder brother had arrived in the city, escaping the Pakistani soldiers further east who had bayoneted their parents and raped their sister. As Bishu was fond of telling everyone, the insufficient meals in the refugee camp, the hunger and the constant anxiety had wrecked his metabolism. However, a barley syrup, prescribed by a homoeopathic doctor and prepared by his wife the previous night, seemed to have finally done the trick, and even before he had woken up that day, he had felt an undeniable stirring in his lower abdomen that promised a release he had not experienced in years.

The pond was completely choked with water hyacinths. It had originally belonged to the local landowner, but after the swarm of refugees settled all around it, the pond became communal property, and was therefore collectively exploited and polluted. Early in the morning, many others from the slums, like Bishu, came here to perform their ablutions. There was no toilet in their shanties or the area. And, later in the day, women would wash their clothes or utensils, or even bathe in the same water. A year ago, the denizens of the area observed the first water hyacinths in the pond, and soon enough, it had overrun the water body, killing all the fish, monopolising the water. Some said the invasive plant had been introduced by the erstwhile landlord: if the pond were of no use to the squatters anymore, he would be able to sell it off to builders, who could then fill it up and construct a multi-storeyed building. Deprived of a source of fresh water, some of the squatters might even move away, allowing the landlord to reclaim some of the plots.

These were not the thoughts that occupied Bishu's mind that morning. Instead, filled with an overwhelming alacrity, he pulled up his lungi, lit a beedi and balanced himself precariously on his haunches at the foul-smelling spot, which served as the communal cesspit for his neighbours with more regular bowel movements. His sphincter had just begun to relax when he saw it. Caught in the water hyacinths was a body. At first, he thought it was an animal, but as he bent forward to get a better look, Bishu realized he was staring at a human body. He could even recognize her: it was Kumkum, the teenage daughter of Bihari migrants who had recently settled in the area.

A strange shiver went through his body as he realized that his constipation was back in full force. Standing up, he tried to shout, only to find that his voice was choked. A minute later, he recovered and screamed out: 'Murder!'

TWO

Ashutosh always said it was futile to investigate an isolated murder in this era of genocides.

I don't know what you know about how we work, but in the police, the boss is always right. Ashutosh was my boss, so I never told him what I thought of his pet philosophy. Initially, my impression was that he, like so many other officers, was trying to avoid unrewarding investigations that comprised the bulk of police work. But soon enough, I realized that was not true: Ashutosh never let files accumulate on his desk, never hesitated from pulling long hours or even working round the clock, and when he was on a case, he was like a hound that had smelled blood.

What? What? Yes, yes, I know the comparison is trite; what did you expect? To want flowery language from a policeman is stupid. My narrative is likely to be full of such descriptions, and if you don't like it, I am sorry I really can't help you there. What I'll give you are facts. Non-negotiable, indisputable. Do what you want with them; they are of no use to me. At times, I will also tell you things which you might find unbelievable or you might feel sceptical about my ability to know certain details. You see one uses one's imagination to reconstruct some events that one might not have necessarily witnessed. It is not fiction, only well-informed guesswork.

Where was I? See what you did with all your questions and doubts? I'll have to request you to not interrupt me when I'm talking. You can ask me what you want when I take a break to smoke or something, but if you interrupt me when I'm talking, I'll lose my train of thought, and these days, it has become very difficult for me to get back to what I was thinking. *Scatterbrain*: that's the word they have been using to describe me these last few months. It's an accurate adjective. The thoughts in my brain are scattered around like grain for pigeons. Or perhaps, they are like the birds, startled, taking flight all at once, in dumb circles.

Let me try again, and don't interrupt.

I reported for work at 10.30 a.m. at the detective department on 13 March 1989, and was summoned to ACP Ashutosh's office half an hour later. Before knocking and entering, I stood for a moment outside, to take a deep breath and brush my uniform. My left eye had been quivering for the past few days and I'm suspicious about these things. What also contributed to my unease was the sound of a woman's laughter from inside. I knocked and was promptly granted permission to enter.

Ashutosh was not behind his table but at the sofa set near the windows. He occupied the single seat, while Rukmini Bose and Muzammil Ibrahim shared the double. She sat closer to Ashutosh.

What? Did I know them? No, no, that was the first time I saw them and Ashutosh provided a brief introduction: Rukmini was a social worker and the director of an NGO that campaigned against child labour. She was also, as I would later learn, Ashutosh's friend from university. Though I was not looking at her directly, I could immediately tell she was strikingly handsome, tall, with a strong bone structure, broad shoulders, a full mouth and large eyes. She also had a strong voice – not loud, but confident; unfamiliar with doubt. She was smoking one of Ashutosh's Camels. Muzammil was her assistant.

'And this is Inspector Pradeep Batabyal,' said Ashutosh, introducing me. 'Our best and brightest.'

To me, he said: 'Take a seat. How many sugars?'

The expensive tea set, complete with a cosy and cups for milk and sugar, was laid out on the centre table. Ashutosh was pouring the tea.

'One, sir,' I said.

'Milk?'

'Yes, sir.'

Handing the cup to me, Ashutosh resumed the conversation they had been having. What he was telling them was not new to me – I had heard it several times before, and had, privately, named it the Theory of Two Motives.

'It is always either of the two: love or money.'

'What do you mean? There are no other reasons for murder?' Rukmini seemed incredulous.

'No, people usually kill for *one* reason: money. Love is rare; and intense love that leads to murder is impossible to find.'

'So, this is the reason you are reluctant to investigate? The inevitable mercenary motive?'

'As usually, Rukmini, you get me wrong.'

The two of them exchanged a smile that was impossible to miss.

'How can I say such a thing?' he said. 'I'm a police officer and I have to investigate crime. But, the thing is, no matter how intriguing a murder looks, the usual motive for it is money.'

'What is your point?'

'Simply this: as a professional, one must be clear-eyed; one must not get distracted by the various confusing strains that inevitably entangle themselves around a crime.'

Rukmini put out the cigarette, though she had only smoked half of it. 'So what is your clear, professional view of what I told you?'

'I have a few ideas, but they are not yet so fully formed that I can discuss them. Maybe you can relate everything to my colleague here, and he will have some ideas.'

'But I have already told you everything.'

'Yes, you have, thank you,' Ashutosh's voice was indulgent, conciliatory. 'Yet, as we have often seen, when people repeatedly narrate a certain set of events, they remember details that may have slipped into some crevice of their memory. These may seem inconsequential to the narrator but are likely to be of immense importance to the listener, especially if they are professionally trained, such as Pradeep and I.'

'Very well then,' Rukmini lit another cigarette.

Pratham Prakash, the NGO where Rukmini served as an executive director, was established about thirty years ago by her mother who was a social worker and a lifelong member of the Congress, and even went to jail in 1942.

Pratham Prakash worked in the Tiljala area. It ran about a dozen evening schools in various places between the railway crossing in the area and VIP Road, further east – a distance of about twelve kilometres. Most of the students in these schools and training centres were children and wives of factory workers. The NGO also assisted municipal schools by supplying books and stationery, and conducting vocational classes for senior students. It had generous allowances from the state and central governments, and some funding from sources abroad. Besides Rukmini and Muzammil, it had three permanent employees, who looked after the administration and finance, and about twenty volunteers on the ground.

'About six months ago, a boy from our school went missing.'

'Name?' I said.

'Anil Kumar.'

'Age?'

'Seven years.'

'Do you remember the date he went missing?'

'It is mentioned here, in the FIR we lodged at the police station.' Rukmini proffered me a piece of paper.

'Thank you, I'll look at it later,' I said, accepting it and putting it on the centre table between us. To prevent it from flying away, I put my cup of half-finished tea on it. 'Please continue,' I said.

She cleared her voice. 'A month later, another student disappeared. Name: Kumkum; age: eleven years.'

Children from lower classes – especially girls on the verge of puberty – going missing was not uncommon. If my memory serves me right, there were about sixty-five unsolved cases lodged with the police in April 1989. The rate of recovery, too, was not bad: it stood at 166. As you probably know, most missing children are kidnapped by traffickers, and forced into prostitution, bonded labour or begging, either in some city or village within the country, or smuggled out through Nepal or Bangladesh. Some have even been rescued from Jordan or Morocco.

'The police are usually quite proactive in such cases,' said Rukmini. (I don't know why but her statement seemed tainted with insincerity.)

She continued: 'These are not the first cases of missing children in the area. With the help of the police, we have been able to rescue almost everyone, including Anil.'

The boy had been abducted by child snatchers. The gang was nabbed by the Bihar police at Motihari. When he was rescued, Anil was traumatized by the frequent beatings his abductors had meted out to keep him subdued. He was also malnourished and in a drugged stupor. But medical care and reunion with his family speeded up Anil's recovery. He was back in school before the end of the month.

'And the girl?' I asked.

'She was found yesterday.' Rukmini's voice remained steady even when she uttered the next word: 'Dead.'

For a minute or two, no one said anything. I could hear the laughter of constables, loud and incongruous, outside the closed doors of the room. Obviously, this information was new only to me; the others in the room were already aware of it. They avoided looking at each other or at me, and I, too, tried to conceal what I felt with a cultivated professional detachment.

The body was found in a hyacinth-choked pond in the area. The exact cause of death was yet to be determined; the post-mortem report was awaited. One thing that Kumkum's parents noticed immediately was that she wasn't wearing any clothes.

Ashutosh and I exchanged glances but Rukmini guessed what we were thinking, and said, 'No, it doesn't look like she was raped.'

The ACP got up from the sofa, walked to the window and lit a cigarette. 'It's all very unfortunate,' he said, 'but what do you want us to do?'

Rukmini put her cup down on the table and slowly said: 'As I was telling you, the police are very helpful when a child goes missing. They take initiative and do their best. But, if a child, unfortunately, turns up dead, they seem to lose all interest in the case.'

Ashutosh was looking out of the window. Now, he turned around to face us. He was backlit and his face was in the shadows; so we could only see him exhaling smoke through his mouth and not read his expressions.

'Can you really blame them?' he said, his voice uncharacteristically flat.

This outraged Muzammil. 'How can you say that, sir? Isn't it the duty of the police…'

'I think I know the duty of the police,' Ashutosh cut him short, 'if you will excuse me, more than you, Mr Ibrahim.'

'What are you trying to say?' said Muzammil, more outraged if that was possible.

Ashutosh was smiling as he replied. 'Please correct me if I'm wrong but it seems to me that you understand English well enough. Was it some particular word you found incomprehensible?'

This combination of bullying and sarcasm would have been enough to shut up anyone else, but not Muzammil. I could not help detect the ferrous core of spunk that allowed him to be completely unfazed.

'Is this the standard operating procedure at the detective department?' he said, returning Ashutosh's sardonic smile.

Resuming his seat, the ACP crossed his right leg over his left. 'We do have a complaints section,' he said, feigning helpfulness. 'Perhaps you could take up my uncivil behaviour with them.'

'Perhaps, I will. You should know that we are not going to let the case drop, and we will not hesitate to approach higher authorities. Maybe, the home minister...'

At this point Rukmini decided to play the referee in the slugfest. 'I think we are getting completely distracted,' she said.

Muzammil wanted to say something but she restrained him with her fingers on his wrist.

'I understand what you mean,' she said, turning to Ashutosh. 'There are too many cases and too few personnel to investigate them. It is a smart move to concentrate resources on those who can still be saved.'

She paused to see if Ashutosh would say something. When he did not, she continued: 'That's why I have come to you. To make a personal request. The girl was my student and I know the family very well.'

'Alright,' said Ashutosh. 'We'll do what we can, but there are limitations.'

'What do you mean?'

'Please try to understand. The detective department cannot take up cases just like that. There is a process. This particular case – accident or murder – is a regular one and should be dealt with by the local police. We have no justification to officially interfere in this.'

'So, you are telling me there's nothing you can do?' A tinge of helplessness was woven into the question.

Ashutosh replied in a soft voice. 'I'm afraid we can't do anything officially, but there are things we can and will do. As I was telling you, Inspector Batabyal is our best. He will look into the case.'

Rukmini looked from Ashutosh to me and back as if she were not convinced. He continued to assure her. 'A local investigation must have already begun. I'm sure we'll have the criminals in custody within a week or so.'

There was a brief pause, after which she replied: 'I'm very hopeful.'

When the visitors had left, Ashutosh stood looking out the window, smoking. I sat ramrod straight, awaiting instructions.

'So what did you think?' he said, at length.

'It could be anything.' I did not want to commit myself right away. 'A kidnapping gone wrong, or an attempted rape. Maybe she resisted.'

'No, no, I'm not asking about that. What did you think of Rukmini Bose?'

I did not know what to make of this question, so I kept quiet. Anyway, no answer was required of me. Ashutosh started telling me of her exploits as a university student and her career in politics during the tumultuous seventies. 'We were not really friends; just in the same batch.'

He sat down opposite me and asked if I wanted another cup of tea, and of course, I had no option but to accept.

THREE

The officer-in-charge at Tiljala police station was not too happy to be summoned to the detective department early on a Thursday morning. He expressed his displeasure by refusing my offer of a smoke or tea, and by shaking his leg impatiently as I looked through the Kumkum Kumari case file.

'Is something bothering you?' I said looking up when the leg shaking did not stop.

'No, no, it's nothing,' he said hurriedly. 'I'm only curious why the detective department is suddenly interested in this case.'

'I'm sure it's just a regular review,' I said in a calm voice and lit a cigarette.

The officer smiled, ironically, and shook his head to indicate that he wasn't taken in by my claim of regularity.

'Why don't you tell me a little bit about the case and how far the investigation has progressed?' I said.

Without demurring, he opened his notebook to the relevant page and began his account:

'A missing person diary for Kumkum Kumari was lodged by her parents on the evening of 10 March 1989. Kumkum was a student of the local municipal school and also attended dance classes organized by a local NGO in the evening. On the day the diary was lodged, Kumkum failed to return from the dance classes.

'The family moved into the area only six or seven months back. They are Bihari migrants from Bhojpur. The father works at a tannery in Tangra; the mother as a maid in some houses on Palm Avenue and East Ballygunge. Kumkum was their only daughter.'

The officer paused as he reached the end of his notes and continued to narrate from memory.

'In such cases, as you know, we cannot rule out the possibility that the girl may have eloped. Kumkum's parents denied it and her friends told us that there was no man or lover in her life. Yet, I continued to stick to this hypothesis because it seemed to me that no one would kidnap the daughter of poor migrant workers for a ransom, right?'

'Quite right,' I said, trying to be encouraging.

'Well, I also thought the kidnappers may have had a different motive,' the officer said. 'Maybe they were not looking for ransom. Maybe they wanted to sell her into prostitution, or maybe they wanted to break her legs or blind her, and make her into a beggar. So, I tapped all my sources and tried to track all the child-snatcher gangs in the city...'

He stopped suddenly, leaving the narrative hanging mid-air.

'And?' I said.

'Nothing.' His voice was tinged with frustration. 'It's as if Kumkum had disappeared into thin air. You know, if a person doesn't want to be found, they can go to extraordinary lengths to ensure that, and even children have a vivid imagination. Anyway, as you know, we failed. Kumkum turned up dead.'

There was a long pause as both of us sat quietly. There was something bothering me.

'Where's the post-mortem report?' I said.

'We don't have it yet.'

This was very irregular. 'Why?' I demanded.

'The doctor wanted a little more time.'

'Why?'

'He was unsure about the exact cause of death. He said it was a heart attack, but he wanted to run a few more tests.'

I didn't understand and asked him to explain. The officer wanted a smoke, so I gave him my pack. He took his time selecting a cigarette and lighting it. Now, it was my turn to shake an impatient leg.

'I don't know how to explain this,' he said, 'but when the body was found, the heart was missing.'

'What do you mean the heart was missing?' I said.

The officer cleared his throat before answering. 'Well, it seems someone surgically removed the heart before dumping the body.'

Later in the day, having recovered a little, I requisitioned all the case files of missing children in the city over the past six months. There were over sixty thick cardboard folders, stuffed with foolscap pages, with single-lined small type running across like endless lines of ants. These arrived in a squeaking steel trolley, pushed into my room by an orderly. Ordering a large kettle of black tea, I lit a cigarette, uncapped my ball point pen, placed it in my notebook, and undid the strings of the first folder. I knew the task I had set myself would take me all night.

You know, this is what we do at the department: ploughing through piles of documents, trying to track patterns and aberrations that might point us in the right direction. People who watch police dramas on TV or read those stupid crime novels seem to think that our work involves a lot of running about, high-speed car chases and adrenaline-fuelled gunfights, but believe me when I tell you, it's hardly ever that. Usually, it's a poor fellow like me, burning the midnight oil, destroying his eyes by straining over the faint type of official documents, and getting cancer by chain-smoking on an empty stomach. And, as far as gunfights are concerned, well, you wouldn't want to be near one. Trust me, I've been in a few.

Anyway, for the first few hours that evening, there was nothing at all. Just the regular stuff: missing diaries and FIRs, ransom demands, arrests, and details of how far the court cases had progressed. Then, finally, just as I was about to give up, I came upon the first case of any interest to me. The similarities between this case and Kumkum Kumari's were so striking that they jumped out of the untidy pile of papers on my desk and hit me on the head.

A ten-year-old girl goes missing. There is no ransom call. The police and the parents are clueless. It seems that she has disappeared off the face of the earth. A few days later, her body turns up. Footnote: the heart was missing. The first case was lodged in mid-November 1988. Between that case and

Kumkum's, three other such incidents were reported from different parts of the city.

A pattern was emerging, and a hypothesis was forming in my head. I remembered Ashutosh's Theory of Two Reasons: there were only two reasons for murder – love or money. Surely, these girls were not being killed and their hearts cut out for the sake of love; there was a mercenary motive. Someone with a more fertile imagination might have come up with ideas of tantric rituals or black magic, but not me. This was my hypothesis: a gang of organ traders was targeting children, killing them, and stealing their hearts. How much would a human heart fetch in the international market? I don't know, but I guess it was enough to motivate these bastards. What troubled me more was that no one in the department had noticed this. The press – usually with a very good nose for such macabre developments – too, seemed to have completely missed it. How long had this been going on? How many cases had gone unreported? How many children were still in the custody of these villains and how were we going to track them down?

By the time I sat down at the typewriter in my office to prepare the report I would submit to ACP Ashutosh, it was already dawn. Providing the details I had unearthed, I recommended an immediate investigation. I also specified my suspicion that a gang of organ traders was operating in the city. As most of the bodies were found in the southern parts, I concluded that it might also be mobile, coming in from Canning or Bangaon, kidnapping their victims and then escaping through the border to Bangladesh, where they might find easy customers. Sealing my report in a thick yellow envelope, I wrote 'Classified' on top of it. It would be a disaster if anyone, especially an enterprising crime reporter, got wind of it. There would be panic on the streets. We needed to make a few arrests before we could go public, and one had to be really careful and discreet as the police department tended to leak information like a broken tap.

As I was thinking of all this, I lit a cigarette and stood at the window of my office, looking out. The crows were making a racket, and a municipal truck was sprinkling water on the streets in an attempt to wash away the dirt of the city.

FOUR

My report on the murdered girls had the same effect on the detective department as a gunshot at a music conference. All through the next morning, the senior officers of all the departments – crime, forensic, and even traffic – were summoned one by one to DCP Biswajit Mukherjee's room, where they remained cloistered for hours. ACP Ashutosh was also there. Before going in, he called me and said, 'Don't disappear – stay where we can find you. You'll be called in any moment.' Then, dropping the half-smoked cigarette on the dirty floor of the corridor, he put it out with the tip of his shoe, and said, 'Good job!'

Following the boss's instructions, I sat in an uncomfortable, cushionless wooden chair in my room and read *Anandabazar Patrika*. The main news of the day was the flood in Orissa, caused by a monstrous cyclone. The army had been pressed into rescue operations. In other news, East Bengal had trounced arch-rival Mohun Bagan three-nil in a friendly pre-league match, but the rowdy supporters of the club had taken their celebrations to the streets, attacking commuters and burning buses till the police was forced to fire tear gas shells to disperse them. Tucked in amidst all this was a short piece about the private militia of upper-caste landowners attacking a village of Dalit sharecroppers in Bihar. The incident was more than a week old and the details were sketchy. The report mentioned that fourteen men in the village had been dragged out of their homes in the middle of the night, lined up, and shot down. The killers had set fire to the thatched huts of the villagers and escaped in boats.

There was nothing else of much interest. So I folded the newspaper and lit a cigarette. It was a stuffy morning, and despite keeping both the overhead and table fans going at top speed, I could soon feel my shirt sticking to my back with sweat.

This was a shame, really, because I had worn my best shirt that day – ironed. I was looking quite smart – even if I say so myself – in anticipation of being called into the meeting with the senior officers. By the time I was finally summoned, long after lunch, my collar had wilted and large brown spots of sweat had formed in my armpits.

It was surprising to find only DCP Mukherjee and ACP Ashutosh in the former's office. I had imagined that the entire top brass of the department would be there, and it was disappointing to not find them. I kept standing even after saluting the two senior officers; they did not ask me to sit. The first thing DCP Mukherjee wanted to know was if I had shared the information with anyone – colleagues, or my wife.

'Of course not,' I replied. 'As you know sir, I am not married, and I thought it would be best for my seniors to decide on this rather than take a hasty initiative myself.'

'Very good,' said DCP Mukherjee. 'You must realize, none of us are heroes here. We are only professionals and all our work is a team effort.'

He launched into a monologue, trying to impress on me the necessity of absolute discretion, and how the press must not get wind of it till we had arrested the culprits. There was no guarantee of how the newspapers would report it; they would probably write about it with a lot of spice and a fair bit of misrepresentation and exaggeration, leading to panic on the streets.

'We don't want that on our hands, do we?' he said.

'No sir,' I replied, like a good schoolboy.

The plan that the bosses had made was actually quite simple. We would track down each and every illegal organ-trading gang in Bengal, Bihar, Assam, Orissa, and Bangladesh. It would involve a fair bit of coordination with our counterparts in those regions, but once we had some of the gang members in custody, surely we could extract a confession. Now, the tricky part was that organ trade wasn't really illegal. There was a thriving business in kidneys and livers, and some of the bigger syndicates enjoyed political patronage, as they contributed generously to the coffers of both the ruling and the opposition parties. So, we would have to be careful about not stepping on anyone's toes, not harassing the legal operations – unless we were absolutely sure of their involvement and had material evidence to back up our suspicions. A team led by ACP Ashutosh would embark on the investigation immediately. Since I was the one who stumbled upon this, I would also be a part of the investigating team. DCP Mukherjee said the last words like a teacher offering a good conduct medal to a mediocre student. Yet, his patronising bothered me less than something else.

'We are going to have only one team?' I asked. It was difficult to curb the incredulity in my voice.

The senior officers looked at each other and ACP Ashutosh shrugged. 'I guess there's no harm in telling him now,' he said.

DCP Mukherjee nodded his head and Ashutosh began to explain. There was already another team investigating a similar case. A month ago, a group of migrant workers had reported that they had been lured to Calcutta with promises of high-paying construction jobs. The night they arrived, they were taken to a hotel near Howrah and treated to a feast, with much eating and drinking, after which most of them passed out. When they woke up a few days later, they realized they had been operated upon, and had severe pain in their stomachs. A medical examination revealed that their kidneys had been surgically removed. This was not the first time such a thing had occurred, but the press had got wind of it, which led to a number of articles, even in international magazines, criticizing the inaction of the police. So a team was formed by the detective department to investigate the case – but it had not met with much success yet.

Coming out of the meeting, I lit a cigarette and stood on the second-floor balcony. Too many thoughts jostled inside my head, like the throngs of petitioners and complainants, the summoned and the hangers-on, in the many bureaucratic rooms right behind me. There was so much noise that I could hardly hear myself think, and suddenly, I felt rather claustrophobic and dehydrated. It must have been all the cigarettes I had smoked since the morning, and the endless cups of tea.

Looking down on the thoroughfare below, I saw an old woman on the opposite footpath, selling green coconuts. Coconut water is considered to be a remedy for dehydration and its pulp is refreshing, so I decided to have one. As I bargained a price with the seller, my uniform providing me undue advantage, I observed that the woman was hunched with her back to the outer wall of a building, covered with decades of official apathy and dirt. The wall got a fresh coat of paint only for political graffiti, and at present, it sported the large red hammer and sickle of the Marxists. The woman, toothless, was herself wielding a crescent-shaped machete, dexterously cutting off the heads of coconuts and offering them to her customers, who sucked them dry with plastic straws and threw the empty shells on an ever-increasing pile, a few feet away. When I paid her, the woman stuck the few coins into her blouse, and, turning her head away from me, spat a mouthful of tobacco juice in a parabola, landing on the pile. And, suddenly, for some inexplicable reason, a brown film covered my eyes, and I had what could only be described as a vision.

This is what I saw: piles and piles of – not coconuts – but human heads. From Howrah to Salt Lake, from Sovabazaar to Bansdroni, punctuating every thoroughfare, every traffic signal, and the ubiquitous garbage dumps, were human heads – men, women, children – all cut off cleanly, just at the neck, their expressions frozen: bewilderment; horror at their fatal destiny; and more horrifyingly, smiles of apathy and ignorance. How could I explain this? It is now impossible to tell, and my memory is too muddled to recollect and analyze what was essentially a momentary, out-of-body experience.

The reverie was broken by a commotion down the road, a car grazing another, and the drivers, quick on the draw, describing in vivid detail what they would like to do to each other's mothers.

FIVE

Why did Ashutosh's drinking problem escalate so much that he started getting into brawls and bar fights with alarming regularity? Why had he and his wife, Sunita Jha, filed for divorce after being married for nearly a decade? Did he cheat on her or did she take a lover? Was Ashutosh, like some of the other officers in the department, hooked on to narcotics as well? These were the questions I had been asked to find answers to when I was transferred to the detective department as Ashutosh's deputy a few months back.

At first, I had thought the promotion was a reward for my swift work in the Camac Street double murder case. An old couple, who lived in one of the large, old houses on the street, had been found dead by the newspaperman one morning. He had gone in to find out if something was wrong, as the newspapers he was delivering had remained uncollected on the veranda for more than a week. Initially, the regular servant of the house was the prime suspect. He was missing, and so were the colour TV and some other electronic devices. But, in the course of my investigation, I found that the old man's son, who lived in Bombay, had been insisting that his father sell the house to a property developer. He needed the money as he had incurred huge gambling debts at the races. We tracked down the servant to his village, and with a little pressure he confessed to the crime. He also told us that he had committed the murder with the active encouragement of his employer's son, who had promised him a handsome reward once the house was sold. The charge-sheet was filed in court within a fortnight, though the son slipped through our net, escaping to Dubai.

For the first week at the detective department, I walked around like I had gained two inches in height and my chest had grown a few inches wide. Yet, soon enough, my misconceptions were dispelled and I was cut down to size when DCP Mukherjee summoned me to his office and briefed me about my surveillance duties. What I had thought was a success was evaluated by my seniors as a failure, and they moved me from external investigations to internal surveillance.

'We don't want any dirt on Ashutosh,' said DCP Mukherjee, as I stood in his office. 'He is one of our most promising officers and we don't want to lose him. We are only trying to help out, do you understand?'

I said I did but the senior officer continued to explain. 'We give our lives to the department, and naturally, the department looks after us, lending us a helping hand if we are in trouble. That's all we are doing here, do you understand?'

Yet again, I indicated that the instructions were crystal clear but it did not seem to impress him at all. Advising me to be discreet, DCP Mukherjee dismissed me. A week later, I got a confidential memo, instructing me to submit a weekly report on the progress of my surveillance.

My first report painstakingly listed details about Ashutosh's marriage and its disintegration.

He had already cleared his IPS training when he met Sunita in 1980 in New Delhi, and they decided to get married. How and where they met and what their parents thought about the match is irrelevant. In brief, there was no opposition from any quarter – they were from the same caste after all, though Ashutosh preferred not to use his surname. For seven years, in sickness and in health, they lived together in different places – Bokaro, Jamshedpur, Dhanbad – wherever he was posted. She had trained to be a schoolteacher and could find a job wherever she went with her husband. After settling in Calcutta in 1987, they decided this was a good place to bring up children. So, Sunita tried to get pregnant but without any success. As they were not getting any younger, they decided to consult doctors, who, after conducting a number of tests, let the couple know their verdict. Ashutosh's sperm count was too low for him to be able to make anyone pregnant. They were told they could think of adoption or surrogacy, but the news had a catastrophic effect on their relationship. Wrapped in their own sorrows, they started to drift apart. Ashutosh spent more time in the office, taking on more cases than he needed to, doing double shifts and making remarkable progress in his career. Sunita, who had so far abstained from giving private tuitions, took on a few students, so that her evenings would be occupied and she had good reason to stay away from their two-bedroom flat in Dhakuria.

Then Ashutosh found out that Sunita had a lover.

To conduct an extramarital affair in this city and keep it discreet was impossible, and soon enough it was apparent to everyone. Only Ashutosh had remained in the dark for the longest possible time.

Sunita's lover was a middle-grade official in the Food Corporation of India. His name was Aurobindo Ghosh. He was an unremarkable man, unambitious, and as middle age crept up on him, he became even more mediocre and ordinary, if it was possible. His wife had died three or four years earlier of a sudden heart attack. It ran in her family. Now, he lived with his twelve-year-old son, Rahul, in a small rented flat near College Street. Rahul was a student at St Helen's High School where Sunita taught history, civics, and geography. Like his father, he was an unremarkable student and had failed in Sunita's subjects that year. So when Aurobindo met Sunita for the first time at a parent-teacher meeting, he requested her to give his son private tuitions. It was an offer she did not turn down.

Soon enough, everyone who knew them started observing subtle changes in their schedules and behaviour. Aurobindo started leaving work at least half an hour early every day. When Rahul would return home from school, he would find his father waiting for him, at least three days a week, with lunch served on the table. Often, Miss Jha, as he called Sunita, would come directly to their home from school and have lunch with them. Then, they would encourage him to go out and play cricket with the other boys in the neighbourhood, while they stayed at home watching TV – or so they told him when he asked them what they would do.

But Rahul was not a child to be fooled easily. He had peeked into the biology books for senior students in the school library and he had a fair idea of what a man and a woman might do together. His suspicions were confirmed when his father told him one evening that he would be going on an official tour and Rahul would be staying for a few days at his aunt's. This was a first. Rahul had never heard of his father going on tours. He had a hunch, which became stronger when he found Miss Jha missing in school for the exact duration of his father's tour.

So, the next afternoon Miss Jha was at their home, instead of going to play cricket as usual, he lingered for a while in the lane outside before returning. But he did not go to the front door and ring the bell. Instead, he stole round to the back of the building, in the dirty alley that separated it from the next house. There was a dead kitten in the lane and it was stinking, but he did not care as he was too excited. He knew that the Venetian blinds of the bedroom windows did not shut properly, and so, bending down a little, he looked in. At first, he could not see anything in the dark but then two human bodies became apparent: his father and Miss Jha. Both of them were completely naked. He was sprawled out on the bed and she was sitting over him, just below his ballooning paunch, moving slowly, letting out cries that Rahul could not even imagine.

He felt a sudden prick in his groin and he knew immediately that he would not go to play cricket in the afternoons Miss Jha was over.

What? What? There you go interrupting me again. How would I know how Ashutosh found out about Sunita's affair? It is impossible to keep something like this hidden for too long from someone as smart as him. Maybe one of his sources tipped him off about the suspicious movements of his wife; maybe he spotted them somewhere. The thing is, he found out. Why do you suppose I know everything about the case? There are details which often slip through, and one must use one's imagination to reconstruct the chain of events. It doesn't mean what I'm telling you is fiction. This is how it all probably occurred; only, I haven't been able to confirm it from individual sources.

So what did he do? Well, his first instinct – and I have this from the horse's mouth – was to take his service revolver and go shoot them. Avenge the dishonour. What else is a man expected to do? Have you seen that movie *Ye Rastey Hain Pyar Ke*? It has Sunil Dutt, Leela Naidu and Rehman. Sunil Dutt is a pilot married to Leela Naidu; she has an affair with Rehman. When Sunil Dutt finds out about it, he shoots Rehman. The plot of the film is based on the famous Nanavati case. You know the jury let the husband go scot-free? They thought he was doing the honourable thing, can you believe it?

Well, Ashutosh didn't kill Sunita or her lover – they are still alive aren't they? He sat in his office, staring at his revolver for a long time, thinking and brooding. Then, he started laughing, lit a cigarette, and decided to go get drunk.

As you know, along Central Avenue, all the bars – Chung Wah, Duke, Arhan Thai, Embassy, Mansukh – have taken to live singing to attract customers. When we were growing up, back in the 1960s, it was only restaurants and bars on Park Street that had singers and performers, jazz and cabaret. Our parents never took us there. It was the playground of the rich and famous; middle-class Bengalis couldn't afford to go to those restaurants, and even they if could, they wouldn't. Now, the Park Street bars have mostly stopped with the singing and dancing, but the cheaper, more disreputable ones in central Calcutta have taken up the baton. Of course, as you can imagine, the crooners here don't perform jazz or rock or even Madonna; the usual musical fare is Bappi Lahiri and Laxmikant-Pyarelal. As dance bars are illegal in Calcutta, these women don't really dance, but they are not averse to shaking their hips with the active encouragement of the management of these establishments.

What? Of course, the police know all this. Why do you suppose our department is considered second only to the Scotland Yard? But sometimes, we've just got to turn our heads and look the other way. What do you suppose these women are going to do if we shut down the bars? Most of them would sink to Harkata Gali or Sonagachi, or even take to shoplifting, smuggling or child trafficking. Who's going to take the responsibility for that?

Anyway, that evening, after driving around the city for an hour or two in his service jeep, Ashutosh turned up at one of these bars. To be specific, it was the Embassy on Lenin Sarani. The reason he went there was the singer. Well, they had two or three singers, but the most popular one was called Sunita. (Yes, the same name as his wife. No, she had no surname; such women often don't, isn't it?) According to my sources, she was one of Ashutosh's informers.

Whether or not he went there that evening to meet her is not clear. Perhaps, there was some information she wanted to give him, or perhaps he utilized her other services, you know what I mean? He arrived long before her performance slot and sat in a corner, drinking. We have also been able to acquire a list of the food he ordered: two plates of fish finger and a foo young. And, eighteen shots of whisky, 60 ml. There is no mention of soda or mineral water in the bill, so we might imagine that he was drinking it on the rocks or neat. One of the eyewitnesses who saw him that night said he was sitting at a table in a not-too-well-lit corner, near the toilet. The table was unpopular as the stench from the urinals hit you directly if you sat there. The only way one could discern that it was occupied that evening was by the cigarette smoke emanating from the corner.

At the restaurant, he was not the only admirer of Sunita's talents. When she came on to perform around 11 p.m., she was greeted with loud cheering from her regular patrons. She was wearing an orange sari, with sequins that accentuated her ample figure. A consummate performer, she acknowledged the cheering – and some catcalls – with grace, tilting her head a little, and immediately launched into the first number. Her performances have often been described as magical. To put it simply, she cast such a spell over her audience that no one would leave as long as she sang, and she usually sang for two to three hours at a stretch. A clear-eyed observer has reported to me that she was not particularly good and there was no great skill or talent in her performance. Her popularity was perhaps due to the fact that by the time she came on, most of the people in the bar were already drunk and not very discerning in their intoxicated states, and the more she sang, the more they drank, getting trapped in the vicious cycle.

That night, more and more people kept coming as Sunita sang. Not only were all the tables filled, some of the larger tables were occupied by complete strangers sitting together, sharing their food and drink without any inhibition. There were also people standing at the bar, around the entrance, at any free spot, glass in hand, calling waiters by waving fifty-rupee notes, ordering for their drinks. The waiters, most of them quite drunk themselves, ran from one customer to another, mixing up orders so democratically that no one really cared what they drank, and as whisky followed rum and vodka followed gin, people got more and more intoxicated and wild.

'I was getting a bit worried that the crowd might go out of control,' said Bahadur Singh, the old guard of the restaurant to me, later during my enquiry.

The trouble began around 1 a.m. By then, Sunita wanted to pack up. As her regular audience knew, when she started singing ghazals, it was goodbye and goodnight. Some of them even started asking the waiters to get their bills. But there were others who were still thirsty – for liquor and also for Sunita's magic. Particularly restive was a gang of boys from the Hindu hostel. There must have been about twelve or thirteen of them and they had come in and occupied the largest table in the restaurant in the late afternoon. Since they had been ordering continuously, the management had not asked them to leave, but by this time at night, the boys were so far gone that they were getting into altercations with the people at neighbouring tables and creating complete pandemonium.

'It was only the intervention of the waiters that prevented an escalation,' recounted Bahadur.

Despite repeated requests from the manager, the performers and even Sunita herself, the boys were not ready to stop having fun. Finally, having had enough of their nonsense, Sunita put the microphone back in its stand and started to get off the stage, to loud protests from the gang. One of the rowdier boys got on stage and held her hand and started to pull her, cheered on by his companions.

'It was my job to intervene but I was scared that they would turn on me and I would not be able to take on all of them,' said Bahadur.

He did not need to. Ashutosh got up from his corner, walked up to the stage, caught the boy by his collar and slapped him so hard that he went stumbling back to his table. The gang had not expected this and they were taken back, but only for a moment. Four or five of them charged towards Ashutosh. At any other time, he would have been good enough for the whole lot of them, but he was also drunk and they managed to overpower him, and started raining blows and kicks on him.

But Ashutosh is a tiger, you know, and when you face a tiger, you don't try to corner him. You run for your life. How long could they keep him down? A minute, two? He was back on his feet, albeit a little unsteady, but his service revolver was out and pointed at them. The boys had not accounted for this, or they were too drunk to realize what they were doing, so a few of them decided to take on the ACP again.

'We heard a shot,' recalled Bahadur.

For a minute, no one moved; no one had a clue what was happening. Then, Sunita collapsed on the floor without a sound. The bullet from Ashutosh's revolver had pierced her heart. In the ensuing chaos, everyone ran for the exits, trampling over the slower, more drunken ones, turning over tables and chairs, and breaking plates of food, glasses and bottles full of liquor.

'When the crowd had left, I saw Ashutosh sitting in a chair near the body,' said Bahadur. 'His nose was bleeding and he was shaking his head.'

Looking at the guard, the ACP said, 'Call the police.'

He lit a cigarette and started to take slow sips from his glass of whisky. Putting a finger in the glass, he fished out a cube of ice and held it to his nose to stop the bleeding.

SIX

The first arrests in the organ-trading case were made on 17 April 1989 – by the other team. They had been investigating the case for a few months and had a headstart. You know, when there are two teams in the department investigating the same case, there is more competition than cooperation. Till ACP Ashutosh and I were assigned to the case, our colleagues in the other team had nothing – no suspects, no arrests, and only a few reports that no one seemed interested in following up. Yet, within a week of my report, they had made an arrest and extracted a confession.

Now that I think back on it, I can't help laughing at how stupid we were. It's all perhaps a result of the utilitarian training we get as cops, to be straitjacketed into those uniforms. Or like those horses on racing tracks, our vision is restricted; we see only what's in front of us and nothing else. We could not even have dreamed of what was afoot.

It was a Wednesday morning when an urgent phone call from Ashutosh woke me up. I had stayed up the previous night, drinking and reading all the reports on illegal organ trade that I could get my hands on. So, in my semi-conscious state, I imagined the ringing of the phone to be a school bell and felt acutely anxious about being late to class.

'Still sleeping?' said Ashutosh when I finally managed to stumble out of bed and stagger to the living room to answer the phone. 'Get your ass here now. We've got our man.'

'Who?'

'The diabolical doctor – the thief of schoolgirls' hearts. He's hanging upside down in the interrogation room. If you get here fast, maybe we can ask him a few questions before he is taken to court.'

This information jolted all the grogginess out of my system. 'Are we sure this is our man?' I asked.

'He has confessed,' said Ashutosh, coolly. 'DCP Mukherjee wants a press conference at 6 p.m. You have to be there, so remember to shave.'

For a moment, I stood rooted to the spot, forgetting to replace the receiver in the cradle. This was incredible and also little disappointing, as I had already started knitting hopes of recognition – may be even a medal – through this case. My reverie was interrupted by the real bell of the municipal school in the neighbourhood.

In half an hour, I was on my second-hand Bajaj scooter, my head in the crushing grip of a hangover, throbbing to the rhythm of the engine. I was on my way to the detective department where I would learn all about how the case had been solved.

Jonathan Chang's family had lived in the same three-storied house at Tiretta Bazaar, not too far from the temple of Tong Achi, for four generations. Like almost all Hakka Chinese families, they too had been in the leather business till labour problems made it impossible for them to continue. So, the family trust – set up by his father and comprising his cousins – decided to sell off their tanneries to a Marwari businessman, take whatever money they could get and emigrate to Canada or Australia. Chang did not leave. He'd been born in Calcutta, had a PhD in medieval Bengali history, and with the money he got from the trust, he could live comfortably in his airy, second-floor flat for the rest of his life.

The top floor of the building was now a restaurant called the Red Dragon, popular on weekends. The ground floor used to be a dental clinic earlier, but now a Bengali doctor had bought it and converted it into a pathology laboratory. Life had continued with only minor disturbances and irritations for Chang till a week back. A heavy downpour had led, invariably, to waterlogging outside his house, forcing him to stay indoors, disrupting his regular visits to the library. To add to his discomfort, his flat was filled with the obnoxious smell of rotting meat.

At first, he suspected the restaurant of not disposing of its garbage properly. But when he complained to the management, they told him that they too were suffering as the odour was keeping patrons away. Then, their attention turned to the laboratory downstairs, which had remained shut for a week. Suspecting the foul smell suggested foul play, Chang called the police.

The owner, Dr Sushovan Sengupta, could not be traced. His flat at Kankurgachi was locked and neighbours said he had gone to Darjeeling with his wife. With no other option, the police broke down the front door of the laboratory and discovered the source of the malodour. Some water had seeped into the ground floor of the building from the waterlogged street outside and caused a short circuit, shutting down the refrigeration unit. In the freezer, the police found not only samples collected for pathological tests but also packets of blood and human organs – livers, kidneys, and a heart – carefully preserved. Without refrigeration these had all started rotting. Since the clinic had no licence to store or trade in human organs, the police acquired an arrest warrant for Dr Sengupta. The investigating officer marked a copy of the FIR to the detective department, where it caught the eye of Manoj Banerjee, an officer in the other team.

'We were already coordinating with the Bihar and Orissa police, but the fucker managed to go only as far as Burdwan. He was holed up in a small hotel near the railway station. His wife was not with him; she disappeared after he told her why they were on the run. She also took all the money they had. Dr Sengupta was actually relieved to be found and arrested – without any money or possibility of escape, he was quite desperate.'

The last part was narrated by Banerjee, who had the irritatingly cheerful demeanour of officers returning from central deputation. He was younger than me, taller, built like a horse, and always sat with his legs spread apart.

'He seems to have confessed to everything,' said Ashutosh. The two-page typed statement was in his hand.

'Oh yes, he was quite forthcoming about the kidney racket. But when we told him about the hearts, he demurred. He kept saying that he had not murdered anyone. But as you know, sir, if you don't let a man sleep long enough and hang him upside down from the ceiling, they'll confess to anything. And if you put a live wire up his dick, he will sing like a peacock.'

'Peacocks don't sing,' I said.

Everyone looked at me and suddenly started laughing, and after a moment of hesitation, I too joined them, though I wasn't sure what the joke was.

SEVEN

Rukmini asked Ashutosh to a Tibetan restaurant in Bhowanipur, popular among couples conducting extramarital affairs. The reason for its popularity was the architecture – a cavernous interior with convenient nooks offering the privacy so essential for such rendezvous. Momo Palace occupied the ground floor of a pre-World War I building. Its unknown architect had mixed elements of Gothic and Baroque, and constructed a series of small rooms. To get into one you had to invariably go through the previous one. As these had only transom windows near the high ceiling, there was very little light and ventilation. The current owners, too, had done very little to improve the situation. The naked forty-watt bulbs hanging in each room hardly managed to make them cheerful, and the whole space stank a little because of the fumes from the toilet and the kitchen.

When it opened in the fifties, the place earned some well-deserved fame for introducing momos and clear soup to the culinary map of Calcutta. In those days, it was not uncommon to see a queue of eager patrons waiting their turn on the pavement outside Momo Palace, especially on weekends. But since then, other places had overtaken it in innovation and quality. The chowmein here had turned greasier; the sweet and sour chicken had lost its zing.

Why she chose this particular venue and why Ashutosh agreed will remain a mystery. Perhaps it was instinctive; perhaps there is a clue in the conversation they had across a grimy, Formica-top table. Here is a relevant extract from the transcription (I have compiled it from the interviews I conducted with the waiters at the restaurant for my report to the DCP):

Rukmini: Do you remember that time we went to Fatehpur Sikri?

Ashutosh: Of course. How could I forget? It was in our final year at the university, right? We took a bus from Kashmiri Gate and stayed at this really cheap and dirty hotel in Agra. The manager of the hotel told us that we should see the ruins in the moonlight, and also arranged for a taxi. All of us barely managed to fit into the Padmini. There was Sunil, Nargis, Madhu – who else?

Rukmini: Francois…

Ashutosh: Oh yes, Francois, our supplier of *malana*, how can I forget him? He went to Zanzibar after completing his degree. Are you in touch with him?

Rukmini: No.

Ashutosh: Where are all our friends? Are you in touch with any of them?

Rukmini: No. Are you?

Ashutosh: No.

(They sit quietly for a bit, lost in their own thoughts.)

Ashutosh: What made you think of that trip?

Rukmini: Look at this.

(She takes out a black-and-white Polaroid and gives it to Ashutosh. It is a picture of them with their friends, all of them squinting at the camera, standing in front of a bus.)

Rukmini: You remember where this was taken?

Ashutosh: On the highway. No surprise that the UP Surface Transport Corporation bus broke down en route. How long were we stuck there?

Rukmini: Four hours.

Ashutosh: Was it really that long? I don't remember, possibly because you entertained us with that ghost story.

Rukmini: Which one?

Ashutosh: It was about a nineteenth-century Bengali bureaucrat posted in Agra. He lives in a haunted mansion and falls in love with the resident poltergeist.

Rukmini: Oh, *Khudito Pasan*.

Ashutosh: What's that?

Rukmini: It's a Tagore story, *Hungry Stones*.

Ashutosh: I think you told us – I forgot.

(For the next few minutes, Rukmini keeps looking at her hand as she talks.)

Rukmini: I guess you have forgotten most things about that trip.

Ashutosh: What are you talking about?

Rukmini: That afternoon we went to Meena Bazaar.

Ashutosh (*Putting his hand on hers*): Of course, I remember. Why would I forget?

Rukmini: I don't know.

(Ashutosh lights a cigarette.)

Ashutosh: I remember everything as if it was yesterday. Staying out in the cold all night at Fatehpur Sikri was a terrible idea for you. You caught a chill which soon became a fever. We were at Meena Bazaar when you suddenly started shivering. I volunteered to take you back to the hotel. I put you to bed in your room, made you take a paracetamol and covered you with three blankets. But the shivering wouldn't stop. So, I got into the bed, under the blankets, and put my arm around you, to warm you. Your skin was burning…

Rukmini: You got hard.

(Pause for a moment. They both laugh.)

Ashutosh: I asked you if you were sure about it.

Rukmini: Always a gentleman, aren't you?

Ashutosh: Afterwards, you fell asleep and I went and sat out on the balcony, reading and having tea. That's where our friends found me when they returned a few hours later. They wanted to know how you were, and – though I wasn't sure of the medical accuracy of it – I told them the paracetamol had worked and the fever had abated.

Rukmini: My memory is now a little fuzzy. What happened after that?

Ashutosh: I remember everything quite clearly. After we returned to Delhi, you avoided me like the plague. It was as if you regretted what had happened between us. Then, I went off for my training, and later I heard that you got married.

Rukmini: I, too, got the news of your marriage.

Ashutosh: We all know how that turned out.

(They remain quiet for almost a minute.)

Rukmini: I'm really sorry about it.

Ashutosh: It's okay – what time is it? Shall I call for the bill?

EIGHT

The humid weather that had gripped the city broke that evening with thunder and lightning. A nor'wester was upon us. When DCP Mukherjee's press conference began at 6.30 p.m., it was still raining outside, albeit less ferociously than before. Almost all senior crime journalists were in attendance, as were senior officers of the detective department. ACP Ashutosh was conspicuous by his absence.

On my way to the press conference, I met Gayatri Vasudevan, the crime reporter of *The Statesman*. She was standing outside the room where the conference was supposed to begin, smoking a cigarette. She was notorious for being rather spunky, never hesitating to ask difficult questions, rushing into crime-prone areas of the city at all hours of the day and night, with little care for personal safety. I had had a few run-ins with her before and did not want to engage with her right then, but she saw me before I could escape.

'Detective Batabyal,' she called out. I had no option but to stop.

'Yes, Ms Vasudevan,' I replied. 'How may I help you?'

'Tell me why we all have been summoned here by the DCP? Have you guys caught some big fish?'

I smiled at her, solicitously. 'I am sure you will get to know very soon.'

'Oh, cut the crap, will you?' She threw her half-smoked cigarette away. 'Where is ACP Ashutosh?'

'I don't know. He should be here very soon.'

'Tell me whom you guys have caught. Give me a scoop.'

I smiled at her again. 'I am sure the DCP will answer all your questions.'

'I get it,' she said, 'you cannot tell me anything. But maybe you can confirm something. Has this press conference got anything to do with the bodies of the dead girls turning up everywhere?'

She had asked the question in a whisper, moving close to me. It hit me like a punch in the gut: how did she know? The expression on my face did not escape her cat-like vigilant eyes.

'Ah, so that's what it is about,' she smiled.

'I really cannot tell you anything,' I muttered and walked away.

The journalists had all come armed with large black umbrellas, which they left in a wooden bucket outside the hall where the briefing was supposed to take place. The bucket had been placed there with the express purpose of keeping the wetness out. But, there was one man who put a spanner in the works. He came in dripping like a wet mop and quietly occupied a seat at the back.

DCP Mukherjee began with a few comments on how the crime rate in the city had come down over the past six months. He then started talking about the illegal organ trade and the efforts of the police to check it. He revealed details from the case of the murdered girls, not forgetting to mention and praise my contribution, and then, with a flourish, he announced that not only did we have a suspect but we had also taken him into custody.

There were excited whispers among the journalists; some complained about not being taken into confidence earlier. DCP Mukherjee said it was a sensitive investigation as they obviously understood – he did not want to compromise it by divulging too much too soon. The questions came thick and fast:

When would the charge sheet be filed? (*The accused was in police custody for a fortnight.*)

Would it be possible to interview Dr Sengupta? (*No.*)

'Of course,' said DCP Mukherjee, 'as I told you earlier, we have a confession from him.'

'Confessions extracted by the police in lock-ups are often rescinded in courts.'

Whether or not this was a question wasn't immediately clear, but it shot into the room like a curare-laced arrow. The one who had fired it was the man who had come in dripping water. He was Caucasian, and I guessed, employed by one of the remaining foreign news bureaus in the city.

'Whom do have I the pleasure of addressing?' said DCP Mukherjee, engaging his interlocutor.

'Tim Taylor, sir.'

'American?'

'New Zealander – though I don't see…'

'Which publication?'

'Freelancer.'

'Right.' DCP Mukherjee lit his pipe deliberately. 'So what do you want to know?'

'I was curious if you are sure that the guy you've got – Dr Sengupta – is actually the same one who killed the girls.'

DCP Mukherjee smiled indulgently. 'Mr Taylor, as I told you, we have a confession.'

'Yes, officer, but the facts are a little strange. Dr Sengupta is an oncologist.'

'So?'

Everyone in the room had turned to stare at him. Tim Taylor, more than six feet tall, was still dripping water.

'Do you suppose an oncologist would be able to extract a human heart for a transplant?' he said.

For a moment, no one said anything. We could hear the rain on the windows; it had returned with renewed vigour.

'I really don't know how to answer such stupid questions,' said DCP Mukherjee. 'Thank you very much for coming. We'll keep you posted about the development.'

Though the journalists had a lot of questions, DCP Mukherjee got up and stormed out.

Slowly and noisily, the hall cleared out. The journalists all left, discussing the details of the case. I stood there, a little short of breath.

NINE

'Would you like to come in for coffee?' Rukmini asked, getting out of Ashutosh's blue Ambassador, which he was driving himself that day.

After lunch, the ACP had offered to drop her home. She lived with her husband and daughter in one of the large houses in New Alipore. By the time they reached, the weather had gone from being stuffy to overcast.

Ashutosh had not expected such an offer. He hesitated for a moment and looked at his watch. It was 4 p.m. He did not want to be late for DCP Mukherjee's press conference.

'I have a packet of Coorgi beans,' said Rukmini.

That sealed the decision. 'Sure,' said Ashutosh, turning off the ignition – not because he was a connoisseur of Coorgi coffee, but because he thought the offer was not only for the beverage.

The drawing room in Rukmini's house was enormous and tastefully decorated. The French windows in its southern wall opened onto a well-kept lawn and garden. Ashutosh could see rows of petunia and marigold, bougainvillea on the boundary wall, and a solitary gulmohar tree in full bloom. The ACP sat on a double sofa right in the middle of the room, under the fan. All the furniture was old and solid, a testimony to the wealth of the family, but muted, aesthetic. Low bookshelves, with antiques and curios displayed on top, ran along two of the walls. In one corner was a large polished piano. But what attracted Ashutosh's attention, as he waited while Rukmini crushed and brewed the coffee in the kitchen, was an impressive shrine on the western wall of the room.

It was dedicated to Yogi Premananda, a yoga guru, who had gained quite a following over the past four or five years. Ashutosh walked up to it to get a better look. The large picture frame had a thick garland of marigold around it and a dozen incense sticks burning in front. The Yogi struck his signature pose in a saffron monk's robe and photochromatic glasses, a slight mocking downward curl to the smile on his thin dark lips. As he looked at it, the ACP recollected all that he knew about the religious leader.

Premananda's ashram on the southern fringe of the city attracted disciples like bees to honey. Many of them were rich businessmen and politicians. It also attracted a large crowd of hippies. According to police reports, gleaned mostly from rumours, there was easy availability of lysergic acid and mescaline at the ashram. Some of the wilder rumours suggested that tantric sex orgies were not uncommon.

'What are you looking at?' Rukmini's voice interrupted Ashutosh's reverie.

He turned around to see her putting down a large silver tray with coffee paraphernalia – pot, sugar, milk, cups, biscuits – on the centre table.

'Did you have to make the coffee yourself?' he asked. 'Where are all the servants?'

'They are all on leave.'

Rukmini lowered herself onto the sofa and indicated that he should join her, 'You didn't tell me what you were looking at.'

Ashutosh hesitated a little before answering. 'Well, I didn't expect to find this at your home,' he said, pointing towards the installation dedicated to Yogi Premananda. 'I never thought of you as particularly religious.'

'I am not.'

'Then?'

'My husband is a devotee of Premananda.'

'Really? I thought he was a doctor.'

'He is a doctor.'

The ACP took a short pause. 'Well, I hope you don't mind my saying this,' he said, 'but I feel it's a little strange to see such a shrine in the house of a man of science.'

Rukmini laughed drily. 'You know officer, the man of science would disagree with you,' she said, giving him a cup of coffee.

'How so?'

'As you might already know,' Rukmini answered, 'the Yogi is an accomplished practitioner of yoga and an expert in Ayurveda. My husband is a great believer in indigenous medicine. He tells me that he often sends some of his more complicated cases to the ashram for a session of yoga, apparently with very satisfactory results.'

By now, Ashutosh had become quite curious and wanted to ask a few more questions, but he did not get the opportunity.

'I think we have spoken enough about my husband and his guru,' said Rukmini. 'Now tell me, what do you think of the coffee?'

'It's better than you promised.'

'Is it? So what do I get?'

At this moment, as Ashutosh would later recall, Rukmini opened her long hair and let it fall around her shoulders.

'What do you want?' he said.

Rukmini smiled and replied, 'Can I have a look at your gun, officer?'

Ashutosh thought he had misheard. Rukmini confirmed: 'Your gun, officer – your service revolver. Could I please have a look at it?'

The ACP hesitated, but Rukmini continued pleading: 'I'll be a good girl.'

She elongated the vowels in a manner that he found irresistible.

'Only for a bit, okay?' he said taking the weapon out of the holster and flipping the safety catch, before surrendering it to her.

'It's heavier than I thought,' she said, pointing it towards him. 'Have you ever killed anyone?'

'Any *one*?' He laughed.

'Is this how you shoot?' Rukmini was still pointing the gun at Ashutosh.

'You couldn't if you tried – the safety catch is on.'

'Then let's make it a little unsafe.' He voice was almost a whisper now. She had turned back the safety catch, revealing that she was not completely unaware of how to use a revolver.

'What if I fired now?'

'At this range, you'd kill me,' said Ashutosh, still trying to keep the mood light.

'And what if I did this?' Rukmini put the muzzle of the gun into her mouth and started moving it as if she were performing fellatio. 'How do you like this?'

The ACP thought things were getting out of hand and lunged for it. But Rukmini was surprisingly quick and leapt out of the sofa, upsetting the coffee pot and spilling all its contents on the expensive white carpet.

Her sari had fallen off her shoulder and was trailing in front of her. Ashutosh was also on his feet.

'I'm sure you like me doing this. I'm sure you are getting hard.'

Satisfied with herself, Rukmini threw her head back and laughed. This was Ashutosh's opportunity. It was all over in less than a minute. He tackled her to the floor, and pinning her down, twisted her arm enough for her to release the grip on the revolver.

The struggle occurred under the photochromatic eyes of the Yogi.

Back on his feet, Ashutosh tucked the gun back into the holster and was about to leave when he heard Rukmini laugh. Turning around, he saw her still on the floor. Her blouse had slid off the left shoulder; the sari had ridden above her right knee.

'Won't you arrest me, officer?'

Ashutosh wasn't sure of what she was saying, 'Where are your handcuffs?' she continued. 'Won't you clap my wrists in them?'

The ACP was still unsure of what she was saying. Lying on her back, not smiling any longer, Rukmini extended her hands towards him. They were joined at the wrists and a little limp, as if she was surrendering to him. Ashutosh took out the iron handcuffs.

Rukmini's hands were restrained to the iron headstand of the double bed in the master bedroom. Ashutosh wondered for a moment if this was the same bed on which she slept with her husband. His expert hands pulled off her sari, her blouse, her petticoat, but as he was about to remove her bra, Rukmini demurred. 'Get into my mouth first,' she instructed.

Hurriedly taking off his boxers, Ashutosh realized he was hard. Rukmini was going to say something, but before she could, he censored her by entering her mouth. Rukmini's skill was undeniable, and yet for the first several minutes, their bodies were all elbows and knees, awkward and hesitant, unable to extract the full ration of pleasure due to them.

Ashutosh pulled out of her mouth, allowing her to breathe, and promptly tore off her bra. He thought her breasts had grown bigger since he had last seen them, or perhaps, memory was playing tricks on him. He eagerly took them in his mouth; first the left one, then the right. In reciprocation, Rukmini sucked in her breath and let out a cry, an almost inaudible one, only for him to hear, and suddenly, their bodies recollected the old, dirty hotel room in Agra and fell into a rediscovered rhythm.

As he entered her, Rukmini looked out of the large window of her bedroom and saw that the skies were the colour of molten lead. It is us that have brought the rain to the city, she thought, though she knew that sudden precipitation was not uncommon at this time of the year. Inside her too, something swelled up, and as Ashutosh went deeper and deeper, all her resistance dissolved, and she made no effort to hold back her tears.

Later, after they were done, and the cloud had gobbled up the city and the afternoon, spitting out darkness and the moist of street lamps, Rukmini went to take a bath. Ashutosh utilized the opportunity to call the detective department and find out how DCP Mukherjee's press conference had turned out.

I was waiting for his call to tell him that the body of another girl had turned up. 'Her heart is missing,' I added.

TEN

The body of Aanchal Agarwal, ten, was found in an abandoned house near Babu Muktaram Street by students of Savitri Girls' College. They were all members of the college dramatic society and had stayed back after classes to attend rehearsals for the annual production. But they could not go home after the rehearsals because of the sudden storm. Not that it bothered them too much, as snacks and cups of tea from the college canteen provided the necessary nourishment for tireless conversation and laughter. Finally, a power cut and an irate canteen owner who wanted to call it a day and refused to serve any more tea, compelled the girls to step out of the campus.

The walk to the bus stop was a short one but it took them longer than usual as they continued to laugh and talk. There were few pedestrians in the area, fewer cars. The Marble Palace appeared on their right, standing like an enormous prehistoric animal in the shadows. Just beyond it was a building rumoured to be haunted. Had they been alone, the girls would have hurried past it. But this evening, with strength in numbers, their pace was relaxed. As they strolled past, they spotted a flickering light in one of the windows. This was highly unusual. As the girls recalled and the residents of the area later attested, the building was always shrouded in darkness. The many claimants to its ownership were engaged in an inter-generational legal battle that had grown incomprehensibly complicated. Earlier, anyone who believed that they had a right to even a square inch of the property, lived in the building, sharing space with fellow residents through some belligerent agreements. However, none were willing to contribute to its maintenance, as a result of which, like many such tenements in the north and central parts of the city, this one too had grown so dilapidated that the municipal corporation forced everyone to vacate it, and hung up a sign warning that the building might collapse any moment.

Later, the girls could not even recall the exact course of events or even why they decided to investigate the source of the light. From what I could gather, it was a stupid act of bravado, a challenge one of them had thrown to the others. It was, in fact, a very stupid thing to do. What if the murderer had still been around when the first girl walked into the building all alone? She, however, returned, running and screaming, barely a minute later. Shocked, she could hardly explain what she had seen, howling, 'Dead!'

The girls accosted a postal department clerk returning home from work down that road, and tried to explain to him what they had discovered. He ran to Mahatma Gandhi Road and convinced an on-duty traffic police constable to accompany him to the dilapidated building.

The constable later told me, 'The dead body was completely naked.'

But that was not the strangest thing. There was a burning candle on her chest, exactly above the heart. It had been placed directly on a pair of stitches marking a cross. As the autopsy later revealed, the heart had been extracted right there; a couple of ribs were missing.

ACP Ashutosh arrived directly at the morgue, still driving his official Ambassador. I was waiting for him and filled him in on the details of the case.

The girl lived with her extended family in a large house on Rowdon Street. Her father was the co-owner of the family business in spices, textiles and iron. The family had come to the city in the middle of the nineteenth century, escaping a drought in Shekhawati. They had accumulated wealth dealing in coal and had then diversified. When Aanchal went missing a week before, the family thought she had been kidnapped for money. They had recently ventured into real estate and were engaged in neck and neck competition with a Punjabi rival who was rumoured to not always work within legal limitations. So they feared he might have kidnapped their daughter to force them out of the deal. They mentioned all this in the FIR but the police found no evidence against the Punjabi promoter. Nor was there a ransom call.

'Rape?' ACP Ashutosh asked the doctor at the morgue who had just finished examining the body.

'No, sir.'

'So, what is it, doctor? Give me your expert opinion. What do you think?'

The doctor took his time to answer, 'In my opinion, it was a perfect cardiac surgery.'

PART TWO

ELEVEN

It took me almost an hour to find the hotel where the journalist Tim Taylor lived, in a blind lane off Sudder Street. I had acquired the address from the foreigners' registration office on Theatre Road and took a taxi to my destination, but I was not really familiar with these parts of the city. This was the hippie central of Calcutta. Though their numbers had diminished significantly since the government tightened the narcotics laws a few years back, those who still came to the city usually found accommodation in the disreputable, rundown establishments in the area, where rents were low and services non-existent.

After roaming the streets for about an hour, I found myself in front of the rusted wrought iron gates of an early twentieth-century building. It was desperately in need of a fresh coat of paint. There was a garden between the building and the road. It had a couple of mango and jacaranda trees. There was no guard or anyone around, so I opened the gates and entered the premises. The garden possibly served as an open-air eating area at times, because there were a few plastic tables and chairs and garden umbrellas around. No one was at the tables, which proved to be dirty on close inspection, and there was no one to serve you even if you took a seat at one of them. One of the garden umbrellas had been uprooted by the last thunderstorm and it lay, unretrieved, by the boundary wall. An abandoned, haunted look hung about the place, eroding my confidence, and in fact, making me doubt the instinct that had brought me here, even as I took the gravel path skirting the garden to the hotel building.

'Officer!'

The cry rang out from the building when I was only a few paces away. I immediately recognized the voice, though its owner remained hidden from me in the shadows of the hotel.

'Mr Taylor, where are you?' I said. 'I can't see you at all.'

Tim Taylor emerged from the shade on the porch where he had been prudently hiding from the midday sun. He was wearing only a pair of Bermudas and his torso was on full display. His feet were encased in local rubber slippers, and in his left hand was a glass half filled with a colourless liquid.

'I was expecting you to come any day, but you took your time, didn't you?'

His voice had a clear, loud ring to it, and as he spoke, he smiled, revealing a set of strong, good teeth. It was rather disarming.

'What do you mean you were expecting me? There was no way you could have known,' I said.

'Oh, I knew alright.' His confidence was jarring. 'Not that it would be *you*, but I have been expecting someone from the police for a week now.'

'Why?'

'Call it a journalist's instinct,' he replied. 'But first, would you like a gin and tonic?' He shook the glass, tinkling the ice cubes invitingly.

It was futile to resist. I climbed the three steps to the porch and occupied an empty bamboo chair. Tim Taylor took the other chair and got busy making my drink. The shade was quite pleasant, and the ceiling fan added to the comfort. Between our chairs was a low table, with the bottle of liquor, a half-finished plate of kebabs and an ice bucket. On the right of Tim's chair was a stack of newspapers.

'Are you the only guest in the hotel?' I asked.

'Currently, yes – there was an entire group of Korean tourists till yesterday.'

Offering the glass to me, and still smiling, he said, 'You guys fucked up big time, didn't you?'

'What do you mean?'

'First, the police tried to hide the murders from the public. Then you caught the wrong guy and tried to frame him. Now you are here because – let me guess – another body has turned up?'

Trying to conceal my discomfort, I said, 'Now look here, Mr Taylor…'

'Please call me Tim, officer.'

'Alright, Tim, let me tell you right away that I'm not at liberty to discuss a case under investigation with a journalist.'

'Right!' He threw his head back and laughed.

'Besides, why do you say we got the wrong man? He has confessed.'

Tim poured himself another drink and fixed his eyes on me. They had a strange penetrative quality. 'Look here, officer, I'm not a rookie scribe whom you can feed a cock-and-bull story. You think I don't know how these confessions are extracted in your lock-ups? You'll be able to prove jack in court and your suspect – that doctor – will be acquitted if he has a half-decent lawyer.' He knocked back his drink and poured himself another.

I took a pause and decided to try a different strategy. 'You would like that very much, wouldn't you?' I said. 'Another story of sloppy police work in a third-world country.'

'Sorry?'

He was a bit taken aback by this sudden offensive, so I continued, 'You think I don't know what Western journalists like you want in India? You want a scoop – a little bit of our poverty, a little dirt, a dash of Mother Teresa that you can peddle back home. Slum tourism, a sort of vicarious pleasure, isn't it?'

The expression on Tim's face was inscrutable. 'When you came here officer,' he said, 'I thought it was because you wanted an exchange of information. But obviously, I was wrong. You can leave, I don't think we have anything to talk about.'

I made a final attempt to tame him. 'You know I can make you a persona non grata. You will be on the next flight back home.'

He gave me a crooked smile. 'I'd like to see you try.'

Are you familiar with the concept of zugzwang in chess? At that moment, sitting on the porch of the hotel, I realized I had worked myself into one. How had I managed it? Possibly because of the aggressiveness inculcated in us during our training. It is good for controlling crowds, or dealing with petty criminals, but for someone like Tim Taylor, tough as a doornail, the strategy was completely ineffectual. What it needed was a subtler touch; a bit of cunning.

I felt the first stirrings of panic rising in my stomach like hereditary gastritis, as I recalled Ashutosh's instructions before he sent me on this assignment: 'Find out everything the fucker knows. Suck his big white cock if you have to.'

'Look Mr Taylor – Tim – I think we started off on the wrong foot,' I said.

'You bet!'

'It's quite obvious that you can help this investigation, so how do you suppose we should proceed?'

'Well, first of all, I think an apology is in order, don't you think?'

'Okay, I'm sorry,' I muttered.

'Now that's more like it,' he said smiling. 'Give me your glass so that I can make you another drink.'

While pouring out the gin and tonic, Tim Taylor said, 'Officer, this is how we will do it. I'll tell you what I know, and you'll tell me what you know – quid pro quo. Agreed?'

Did I have a choice?

TWELVE

Though the terms 'slum' and 'basti' are used interchangeably, Ashutosh knew the legal difference between the two. The first is defined as an area with conditions injurious to public health or morals. Such areas constitute almost half of the city's settlements. By contrast, a 'basti' is a technical term, referring to an area of not less than 700 square metres, occupied by huts or dwellings constructed out of non-concrete material. The distinction seemed simple enough. Yet, the place where the ACP found himself that morning seemed to defy all such bureaucratic classifications.

You might wonder how I know the exact details of what Ashutosh was doing that day. Well, to begin with, he was excellent at keeping notes, which he shared with me, and what he did not share, I could decipher and imagine. What? No, when I say I imagined, I do not mean I am making things up – this is how it all probably happened, but I have not found independent corroboration for it.

Ashutosh parked his blue Ambassador along the back wall of Don Bosco School in Park Circus. The wall was at least ten feet high, and the only entrance was through a large iron gate, always shut and manned by surly guards. The English-medium school represented all the aspirations of the middle classes that needed to be demarcated and protected from its less fortunate surroundings. If you were allowed entrance on the campus, you would encounter a large football field, basketball courts, a manicured garden with gravel paths all around it, the impressive H-shaped building painted a uniform yellow and grey, and another garden with a fountain leading to the formal entrance on Darga Road. Across the road was Park Circus Maidan, the only surviving green stretch in this cluttered area of the city, the only breathing space. In winter, it hosted Russian circuses, complete with menageries of tigers, horses and elephants. The students in their classes on different floors of the school could hear loud growls and trumpets emanating from the large tents pitched by the foreign performers. Some of the more imaginative students speculated on what would happen if a lion escaped its cage and wandered into the campus. But nothing of the sort ever occurred. Not even the fierce lions dared break the discipline and order that were the twin religions of the Catholic fathers who governed the school.

Behind the school wall, where Ashutosh had parked his car, were railway tracks, and beyond that, a network of lanes, inaccessible in cars, comprising the slums of Tiljala, Tangra, and Topsia. As he was locking the car, Ashutosh looked up and saw a large hoarding with the stencilled picture of a rickshaw puller. The caption demanded: *Calcutta, to whom do you belong?*

Crossing the railway tracks on foot, Ashutosh entered the archipelago of huts that could only be described as a sort of grey zone, cut off from the city in the south by a drainage canal and in the north by heaps of garbage. There were no roads here, no civic infrastructure to speak of, the water and electric supply sporadic, and the common latrines dysfunctional. It had not rained for a few days, so the lanes were dry. Ashutosh knew this was a lucky coincidence because after every spell of rain, these would become running gullies of sewage. Now, he only had to skirt the puddle where malaria-transmitting mosquitoes laid eggs. The ACP, however, was not so lucky with the odour that hung in the air – the stench from tanneries nearby that hit the gut like a sharp punch, and was so overwhelming that Ashutosh had to take out his handkerchief and put it over his nose and mouth. This provided only partial relief; he could feel the odour latching onto his clothes, skin, hair, like claws. Pushing his disgust to the back of his mind, Ashutosh walked briskly towards his destination: the office of the NGO Pratham Prakash.

Rukmini had given him exact directions, but Ashutosh found himself quite lost after ten to fifteen minutes. Poverty had cast a spell of tedious homogeneity over the area. All the houses had walls made of tin sheets and roofs of polythene and terracotta tiles. Nearly everything here was painted a shade of blue, sponsored – as he would later learn – by a United Nations fund. It was not a pleasant colour and it stuck to surfaces like grease, dirty and peeling off. This monochromatic monologue was punctuated at regular intervals by graffiti of the red hammer and sickle, or a flag or two of the Marxist party. Ashutosh suspected the uniformity was not accidental. It had been cultivated to discourage curious outsiders like him from venturing too far into these lanes, and if the ACP were not a bulldog, they would not have succeeded. At one point, he thought of giving up the expedition and returning another day with better directions, and maybe also Rukmini as a guide. But, it proved impossible to retrace his steps to where he had parked his car, so he decided to keep going onward, expecting to eventually emerge on the EM Bypass, and hoping that he was not going around in circles.

What struck him as odd was the absence of people. It seemed as if all the denizens of the slum had disappeared overnight or had gone off on a pilgrimage together. Or perhaps, they had retreated into undetectable holes from where they were keeping a close watch on this intruder. All the houses he passed stuck to each other in mute lines, their doors locked and their windows barred. No curious child peeped out at Ashutosh, no woman was spotted hurriedly pulling the end of her sari to cover her head or breasts, no man stood urinating at a wall. The only humans he came across were a gang of adolescent or pre-adolescent boys, four or five of them, playing with a tyre, rolling it along with a small stick. They did not even turn to look at the ACP.

After wandering around for another twenty minutes, he stumbled upon an open space – an unlikely clearing in the forest, where all the neighbouring lanes converged. This was a construction site. Ashutosh was quite surprised to find a concrete building of ample proportions coming up here. It was, however, not a tenement, but something else altogether: a temple. He stood there observing the army of construction workers taking advantage of a dry day in the middle of the rains to get on with their work. The structure, currently mostly scaffolding and jute sacks, was coming up on a pond that had been filled with concrete and rubble. This had become a common phenomenon in the city. Many of the ponds and water bodies in the city were publicly owned and protected by municipal laws, though that did not prevent them from falling prey to developers, who could easily pay off the civic officers concerned. The fate of the privately-owned ponds was way more precarious, as Ashutosh knew. But these were not the thoughts that occupied him at the moment. Something else caused him considerable alarm.

It struck Ashutosh that this could be the same pond in which the body of the twelve-year-old girl was found. As he observed the feverish activities of the construction workers, he became almost sure that this was indeed the spot where Kumkum Kumari's body was discovered. 'Could it have been another pond?' he wondered for a moment, but then decided against it. How many large water bodies could there be in this cluttered part of the city? Ashutosh wondered how the owners had acquired permission to sell off the pond and who had allowed the builders to start construction here. Right in front of his eyes, a crime scene was being contaminated, destroyed; all the evidence it could have yielded was being buried and lost forever. It was essential to stall the construction, at least for a week or so, and the detective department be given access to examine the area.

The thought of the bureaucratic battle necessary for that made Ashutosh feel very tired. No one in the department would support him; instead they would all be up in arms if the investigation was restarted. But how did this gross negligence in procedure take place? Had they turned complacent and lost perspective after arresting Dr Sengupta?

Even as he thought of all this, he leaned against a wall and lit a cigarette.

'ACP Ashutosh, is that you?' The voice was behind him. He had been recognized, despite being without his uniform.

Ashutosh turned around to face Muzammil.

'What are you doing here?'

'I was going to see you,' said the ACP. 'It is good that we met because I have completely lost my way.'

A smile broke across Muzammil's lips. He was wearing khadi trousers, rubber sandals and a checked cotton shirt sticking to his torso with sweat.

'It is not uncommon to lose your way in these lanes,' he said. 'It took me about six months to familiarize myself. But shall we continue in the office?'

Ashutosh agreed readily. As they started on their way, he asked Muzammil if he knew what was being constructed here.

'Yes sir, this is a Vasant Sena temple.'

'Vasant Sena?' The ACP had heard the name before but could not recall it immediately.

Muzammil said, 'The religious organization headed by Yogi Premananda.'

THIRTEEN

By the time I finished narrating to Tim Taylor how far – or rather how little – the investigation had progressed, dusk was already stalking the garden in front of the hotel. I had expected the journalist to take out a notepad and a pencil, but he did not. Instead, he sipped quietly on the gin and tonic and smoked his cigarette. Later, he boasted that he could recall ninety-nine per cent of any conversation he had and reproduce it verbatim on paper even the next day.

'So, what do *you* make of the murders?' I said to him. 'You were very confident that the doctor we had arrested was innocent of these crimes. Was it only because he was an oncologist? Or is there someone else you suspect?'

Tim Taylor did not answer my questions immediately. He relit his cigarette and started blowing smoke rings towards the ceiling fan.

After waiting a minute or two, I prodded him again: 'Well?'

He got out of the chair and, inexplicably, started pacing about. 'What do you think I'm doing in Calcutta?'

'I don't know.'

'Of course you don't. But suppose you had to guess. What do you think a fairly successful journalist from New Zealand is doing in this shithole?'

I was still trying to decide if this was mildly or immensely offensive when Tim reoccupied his chair, relit his half-burnt cigarette, and without preamble, began narrating a most curious story.

Tim Taylor had been in Calcutta for eight months. Before that, he lived in Auckland and was a senior crime reporter for *Auckland Star*. 'Most crime, as you know, is economic,' he said. 'So, I have always had a simple rule: follow the money. More often than not, it would take me straight to the criminals, sometimes even before the police, much to their chagrin. But there was plenty of good humour and it was not uncommon for crime reporters and police officers to buy each other drinks, after duty hours, at one of the harbour-facing bars.'

'How can I describe to you how different Auckland is from Calcutta? Let's just say the streets are cleaner and pavement dwellers don't make it difficult for pedestrians to follow a straight path. Let's just say there are more trees and less dogs and the weather is more tolerable. Let's just say violent crimes are not so ubiquitous that no one notices when bodies of teenage girls, their hearts plucked out of their chests, start turning up with an alarming frequency at street corners and garbage dumps.'

'So, bodies of teenage girls started turning up in Auckland, did they?' I enquired.

'No,' said Tim, 'but something else happened.'

'On January 29, 1988 – a particularly warm day, the height of summer – twelve men and women were found dead in a flat in the Mission Bay suburb of the city. They had all consumed a cyanide solution mixed with fizzy orange juice.

'You realize what a buzz such an incident would have created in our otherwise quiet little town? What a jarring note in the symphony of the unbroken good weather we had that year. Suddenly the skies were overcast with angry storm clouds. At the harbour, the cries of seagulls had grown shrill, discordant.'

'Can we please abandon these poetic metaphors?' I demanded.

'Don't be rude, you insensitive policeman. You don't get – can never get – what a shock it was for us. For more than a week, there was nothing else people discussed at the cafes and bars, at weddings and funerals. The only subject that occupied our thought, our days and nights, our waking hours and dreams, was the collective suicide of those seven men and five women.'

'So did you find out who they were?' I demanded.

Tim poured out another round of drinks. He took a large sip from his glass before answering my question: 'They were all members of the Vasant Sena.'

I almost choked on my drink. 'You mean Yogi Premananda's Vasant Sena?'

'How many Vasant Senas do you know of?'

'I did not know they had branches in New Zealand.'

'They have branches everywhere in the world: London, New York, Paris, Berlin, Buenos Aires, Cape Town, Sydney, Tokyo, and now even in Moscow, where – in defiance of Soviet practices – they have even opened a temple, to which thousands of devotees flock every day. It has turned into a powerful, influential, and at times, even a militant global organization. You can't ignore it.'

That is the exact mistake the authorities in Auckland had committed: they had ignored the small group of sanyasis and sanyasins who had settled in the ranch on the outskirts of the town. They had imagined it to be another hippie, spiritualist fad, like ISKCON or Osho, passing through, like a roadshow or a circus. Their unaccountable popularity and growing number of followers hardly seemed to interest anyone, except the feature writers of the *Auckland Star*, who did half a dozen long-form stories on the exotic religious practices and rumours of drug-fuelled sexual orgies at the ashram.

Tim had a hardcover folder with neatly organized cuttings of these stories, and he read them out to me.

One form of meditation required the devotee to sit cross-legged in front of a mirror, contemplating their past lives. Some of those who tried this asana reported watching their previous births playing out in front of their eyes like a technicolour film, on the surface of the mirror. While some of them saw themselves as exactly they were in this life, others reported a change of gender, ethnicity, language, and even species, turning from human to animal, bird, fish, or even insect. The spokesperson of the ashram explained that this meditation was aimed at helping people understand the concept of maya and get over the sorrow and pain of their current, miserable lives.

Life at the ashram, however, comprised not only meditative practices but also sexual ones, a few of them quite bizarre. One reporter narrated how she took part in an initiation ritual where she needed to have sex with four different men at the same time. She went ahead with it, in a spirit of inquiry and curiosity.

The carnal act had to be performed in front of a small group of devotees, of both sexes, who sat cross-legged and naked. If any of them were aroused by the pornographic performance, they would be confined to a room and forced to fuck multiple partners till they had had a surfeit and begged to be released.

'Is this true?' I asked, shocked.

'Every word of it,' replied Tim.

'But what was its purpose?'

'Apparently, it was very effective in curing sex addicts.'

I could not help an incredulous laugh, but then I remembered something, and my mood grew sombre.

'As bizarre as all this sounds,' I said, 'it still doesn't explain why those people committed mass suicide.'

Yet again, Tim took his time to answer. He filled our glasses and sat quietly, looking out at the garden and contemplating something. From where we sat, we could hear the city coming back to life in the late afternoon, the voices of humans, music from record players, cars, but it was like hearing a distant rumble of the sea. There was no choice but to wait out Tim's silence patiently.

For a moment, my thoughts turned to ACP Ashutosh and where he might be then. Since the last body was discovered, he had come up with a plan: to surreptitiously visit the families of all the girls who had been killed. They had all been interviewed, right after the discovery of each body, by different officers. At the detective department, we had only read these reports and had arrived at our conclusions. It was like the blind men trying to figure out what an elephant looks like by touching different parts of its body. This way, Ashutosh felt, we would never be able to figure out the actual picture. So, he had set out that day to do some good old detective footwork.

'Well, are you going to say something?' I asked Tim after waiting for about fifteen minutes.

'Yes,' he said, taking a long drag on his cigarette that had almost gone out. 'But I am trying to figure out how to begin.'

The twelve followers of Yogi Premananda who drank the fatal potion were among his most devoted. They were convinced that this was the road to nirvana, to be free of their mortal, vulnerable bodies, and to escape all the pain their bodies caused. As soon as they died, a gang of organ snatchers entered the flat and started preparing the bodies for surgery. Who knows how they had planned to dispose of the bodies after the livers and kidneys and god knows what else, had been extracted?

'But how do you know all this?' I interrupted. 'If it was all so well planned, there was no way the bodies would have been found in the flat.'

Tim bent towards me and in almost a whisper said, 'You see, there was a survivor. It was not twelve people who had tried to commit suicide that day, but thirteen. One of them lived to tell the tale.'

FOURTEEN

On their way to the office of Pratham Prakash, Muzammil described to Ashutosh a recent development in the area: the proliferation of Vasant Sena activists and their rising popularity.

Till about a year back, when Muzammil had just arrived in Calcutta from Srinagar, there were three groups that did social work in Tiljala: Mother Teresa's Sisters of Charity, the local Communist Party of India (Marxist) offices, and Pratham Prakash. The aims of all three organizations were unique, and though there was some inevitable overlap in their work, conflict between them was unheard of. On the contrary, there was usually a lot of cooperation and sharing of resources, essential in the enormous task of the uplift of the destitute. Then, about seven or eight months ago, the first Vasant Sena office opened in the area, in a small temporary room, and its saffron-clad volunteers started soliciting membership with some success. This brought them into immediate conflict with the CPM workers, who were ever watchful of any contrary influence in their constituency.

'Of course, as you know, the Party and the Sena have always been against each other,' said Muzammil.

'What do you mean?' asked Ashutosh.

Muzammil was very surprised that Ashutosh did not know about this. 'The CPM has always claimed that the Sena received funding from the CIA and its only objective is to perpetrate a militant and majoritarian Hindu ideology,' he said. 'The Left Front has also accused the Sena of anti-state activities and stockpiling arms. There has, however, never been any proof of these accusations.'

The conflict reached murderous proportions four or five years back: a few monks and nuns of the Sena were attacked on Dhakuria Bridge, assaulted, burned and killed. Though the incident occurred in the middle of the day, no witness came forward and no one was ever arrested, though it was common knowledge that the attack had been orchestrated by miscreants in the pay of the Party. Since then, the evangelic work of the Sena – converting people to Hinduism, cow protection – had been put on the back-burner.

'But a year ago, Yogi Brahmananda, the founder of the Sena, died and was succeeded by Yogi Premananda,' said Muzammil. 'Till then, Premananda had been spreading the message of his guru all over the world. Since assuming charge of the Sena, he seems to have taken a more aggressive stance to expand the support base of his organization.'

'Here in Tiljala?'

'Not only here – if reports are to be believed – everywhere in the state. Since I work here, I have been able to observe their strategy.'

The first Vasant Sena office in the area was humble, non-descript. It was manned by a couple of volunteers who distributed the Sena literature and tried to induct members. You know, though the Sena is a Hindu supremacist organization, they have always been deeply opposed to caste, describing it as un-Vedic. This helped them gain popularity among the large population of migrant workers from Bihar who live in Tiljala. Most of them are Dalits. Being anti-caste is an old strategy for every new denomination or religion in our country. Buddha, Mahavir, Guru Nanak, the first Muslims and Christians – everyone has used it. The Vasant Sena too started reaping the benefits of this strategy and their membership began swelling. Its flag of a half-risen sun on a yellow background started appearing over the roofs of shanties; their numbers had soon overtaken the red hammer and sickle. The number of Vasant Sena offices also grew exponentially. They started hosting yoga classes in the morning and kirtans in the evening. The sermons of their volunteers became more aggressive, highlighting how the CPM had failed the people.

'Then the construction of the temple started, and the conflict escalated.'

Ashutosh interrupted the narrative because he remembered something. 'The pond that has been filled up to make the temple – isn't it the same one where the body of the girl was found?'

'Yes, it is,' said Muzammil.

'I wonder how they got permission to build at a crime site.'

Muzammil did not know the details. 'I have heard that the owner of the pond is a devotee of Yogi Premananda.'

'Is there anyone who isn't?'

Ashutosh laughed as he said this, he had meant it as a joke. But Muzammil replied seriously, 'I'm not – and that's why I have resigned from Pratham Prakash.'

'What do you mean?'

'Did Rukmini Ma'am not tell you? I put in my papers the day before yesterday.'

Rukmini had, in fact, told Ashutosh nothing about it, which he found quite strange. Muzammil explained his reason: 'I cannot continue to work for an organization that subscribes to the Sena's ideology.'

The ACP did not understand, so Muzammil pointed out the office of Pratham Prakash. They were only a few paces from it.

'The epidemic is spreading,' he said.

Ashutosh looked up and saw, above the slanting roof made of terracotta tiles, the yellow flag of Vasant Sena, limp and sinister in the humid evening.

While they were having tea at the Pratham Prakash office, Muzammil told Ashutosh about how the NGO, once uncompromisingly secular, had now decided to align itself with the Vasant Sena. The person responsible for this transformation was Dr Raktim Bose, Rukmini's husband. As the ACP knew, Dr Bose's entire family had been initiated into the Sena and they were great patrons of it since the time of Yogi Brahmananda. Earlier, the Sena followers were discreet, muted in their religious practices, confining it to their homes and ashrams, and occasionally taking out processions of music and dance. But now it seems everyone – ordinary people, neighbours and friends and cousins – has turned into a snarling rabid dog, baring its fangs. Dr Bose was a member of the governing body of Pratham Prakash. He had convinced the other members that the NGO would benefit through its association with Vasant Sena. It would mean more funds, better infrastructure.

'Can you believe it? All these proud secular, social workers selling themselves for a few lakh rupees?' said Muzammil.

His voice was tinged with disappointment as he drained the dregs of the tea in his cup.

'You know, I feel there is no real fundamentalism,' he said. 'No one really hates a Muslim or a Jew. All they care about is the money.'

The reason Ashutosh had visited the *basti* was not to see the office of Pratham Prakash, which he could have done any day with Rukmini, but to meet the family of Kumkum Kumari. The disappearance and death of the girl had alerted us to the case, and the ACP wanted to re-interrogate the family to find out anything the investigating officers might have overlooked.

Muzammil knew where Kumkum's family lived and offered to take Ashutosh there. On their way, they could hear kirtans, accompanied by cymbals and conch shells. The direction from which the sound came remained undetermined, but Muzammil told Ashutosh it would be one of the Vasant Sena offices. The entire settlement seemed to be coming to life now; more people were up and about than when Ashutosh had come in the afternoon. What caught his eye were the numerous outlets of country liquor. Men gathered around these like bees at a honeycomb. The ACP wondered if these were legal, but he did not have the time or the inclination to investigate. The two of them walked at a brisk pace.

Kumkum's family lived in a hovel, indistinguishable from the others in its line. It comprised one windowless room, no more than a hundred square feet in size, which served as the bedroom and the kitchen. The only source of light was a naked bulb hanging from the ceiling by a wire. Even in the little light it emanated, Ashutosh saw a shrine to Yogi Premananda in the cleanest corner of the room. It was a near exact replica of the one he had seen in Rukmini's house, only smaller and less ostentatious.

Muzammil introduced Ashutosh to Kumkum's father, Dashrath Manjhi. A frail man, he was wearing only a lungi and sitting on his haunches, chain-smoking bidis. No introduction was provided for Kumkum's mother who was cooking inside the hut. As the smoke from her stove had filled the room, the three men stood outside.

Ashutosh offered Dashrath a cigarette and got straight to the point: 'I'm here to ask you if there is anything you can think of, anything you can remember that might help us catch the murderer of your daughter.'

Dashrath seemed surprised by the question. 'I thought you had already arrested the doctor for killing young girls and selling their hearts. I read in the newspaper.'

'Yes, we have, but we also wanted to be sure that he had no accomplices.' The ACP tried his best to not betray the faux pas he had made. 'Is there anything you can tell me, any detail, even if you think it is insignificant?'

'We told everything to the officer who came earlier.'

Dashrath's voice was soft, but cold and uncompromising. Its flat tenor refused to reveal any secrets. But the ACP persevered: 'You know, very often when we revisit our memories, we remember things that we may have missed the first time. It is like stumbling upon something we thought we had lost, in a corner of our house.'

Though Dashrath did not smile at this, Ashutosh thought he saw the hint of an ironic curve to his lips. 'My house is very small sir,' he said. 'I cannot imagine who would want to kill my little girl.'

'That is a question we are all grappling with,' he said. 'Since there is nothing you can tell us, can I ask you something else?'

Dashrath did not give his consent, nor did he refuse. He just stood there, smoking.

'Are you a member of Yogi Premananda's Vasant Sena?' asked the ACP.

'Yes, I am.' Again, the cold passivity.

'A lot of your neighbours also seem to be.'

'Yes, they are.'

'I was curious about how you became a member.'

'Why? It is not illegal.'

'No, of course not. But, you know, some thought goes into it before people decide to join such an organization. You must have also thought about it.'

Dashrath dropped the cigarette he was smoking. It fell into a muddy puddle and was extinguished.

'It was last monsoon,' he said. 'We were living on the pavement near Howrah, under tarpaulin sheets. My son had pneumonia. But the hospital would not take him – there were too many patients already. Where could we go? There was not a single dry spot in the whole city for us. Yogiji found us and took us in.'

'Where did you come from?'

'Ara.'

Ashutosh thought he had found a point of entry. Switching over immediately to Bhojpuri, he said, 'We are from the same state, you know. I am from Ranchi.'

Again, Dashrath did not say anything but kept staring at him with those cold, impassive eyes. Was he a heroin addict or was this the numbness of a bereaved father, the ACP wondered.

'Why did you come to Calcutta?' he asked.

Dashrath did not say anything immediately. Then slowly he asked: 'Are you a Bhumihar?'

'Yes.'

'Is that why you hide your surname?'

Ashutosh felt his ears turning hot. He could have slapped the fucker right there. 'No,' he said calmly. 'But what has that got to do with it?'

Dashrath took his time to narrate:

'We came to Calcutta to escape the Bhumihars of our village. They were killing people of our caste, throwing us under tractors, into brick kilns and wells, or shooting us with their old rifles. They would come to our houses and take our women and daughters and we would never see them again. Then, one night, their army set all our houses on fire and killed anyone who tried to escape.

'It all began in the season before sowing the crops. Some labourers from our caste wanted more wages. It was not an unfair demand, they only wanted what the government had fixed. But the Bhumihars did not want to pay even that. The labourers refused to work. The atmosphere in the village was very tense. The zamindar's henchmen started kidnapping the wives and the daughters of the labourers to make them work. There were frequent fights. The police would always come and arrest us. They, too, were Bhumihars after all.

'One night, the zamindar's house was attacked. The attackers killed him and his son and set the haveli on fire. No one knew who did it. It could have been a gang of dacoits or Naxalites. But this gave the zamindar's family and upper-caste men the excuse they needed for retribution. My cousin, Ram, was found dead in the fields, his head smashed by a stone. His brother, Laxman, disappeared, only to be discovered hanged from the branches of a tree a week later. There were many more such deaths.

'The night the army of the Bhumihars attacked our village, coming in silent boats across the river, I had remained sleepless, racked by anxiety. Perhaps that is what saved us. By the time they started setting the first huts on the edge of our village on fire, I had already escaped into the forest with my wife and children.

'We walked all night in the darkness, looking back frequently at the fire and the smoke in the village behind us. By daybreak, we were at the railway station, twenty kilometres away. We hid in the shrubs, waiting for the train. When it arrived, we sneaked into one of the compartments, undetected by the sleepless passengers, and hid in the bathroom.

'That's how we came to Calcutta.'

For a long time after Dashrath finished, no one spoke. Only kirtans and conch shells could be heard in the distance.

FIFTEEN

There was a saptaparni tree in the garden, and the smell of its nocturnal flowers reached us like a telegram through the unbroken darkness cast like a spell around the hotel's premises. No one came to switch on the light, even on the porch where Tim and I sat drinking. The journalist did not hurry with his narrative. Perhaps the slow pace was due to the nature of the events he was about to describe. Their recollection required patience, courage. In the meanwhile, I was getting impatient. I was meeting Tim Taylor so that the investigation could be speeded up, and though it was not unpleasant to sit here, drinking gin and tonic with this athletic man, I really did not have the time to indulge myself.

'Will you tell me the name of the thirteenth person?' I asked.

'Her name was Hope.'

'Hope what?'

'She did not use a surname and we never found out.'

She had, however, given a statement to the Auckland police, and a copy of it had found its way to Tim Taylor's meticulous folder. He let me read it. Here is as faithful a reproduction as my muddled memory will allow me:

Statement of Miss Hope to Auckland police
(Dt. April 30, 1988)

There would be no pain. That's what we were told. The orange drink we would consume was supposed to knock us out before slowly switching off our vital organs. It worked exactly as we were told for everyone but not for me, I don't know why. The poison in the drink was, in fact, strong enough to induce a blackout. However, in about five or ten minutes, I had returned to my senses, retching violently, vomiting all over myself. My head and my limbs seemed to have turned into heavy bricks and my vision was unclear. Violent spasms gripped my body. Somehow, I managed to crawl to the bathroom and shut the door. (I think that saved my life.) Everyone else who had the drink with me was dead; their bodies were strewn all over the carpeted floor of the living room.

In the bathroom, I turned on a tap and tried to clean myself, but I think I passed out again.

How did we end up in that two-bedroom flat, naked, and – well, for everyone else but me – dead? We were indoctrinated, trained and prepared for it. Whenever anyone is initiated into Vasant Sena, they must undergo a thorough medical examination. That's how they chose us, I think. Immediately after my initiation, I was put on a strict regimen: healthy vegetarian diet, yoga, meditation. Now, I realize I was being prepared – like the others. We were being taken care of like cattle for slaughter.

Along with the preparation for our bodies, there was also the preparation for our minds. Yogi Premananda was fond of telling us about maya – the Hindu concept that nothing in this world is real, that everything is a cosmic dream, that pain and pleasure are equally elusive. So, it is futile to attach any importance to any person or thing. In any case, he convinced us that we were not actually going to die – it would be an escape from our mortal bodies, we would achieve nirvana.

So, on the appointed date, all of us were driven to the flat. Before leaving, our escorts made us surrender all our mortal possessions – clothes, jewellery, watches – till we were absolutely naked. There would be no need of these earthly things where we were going. Then they locked the door of the flat and left us. It was still afternoon and we were supposed to consume the drink at midnight. So how could we better occupy ourselves than by conducting an orgy? It was one of the wildest ones I have ever taken part in, and believe me, I have been in a few. Everyone was willing to try anything because this would be it. Later, when everyone was exhausted, we sat in a circle, prayed, and drank the orange juice.

When I returned to my senses on the floor of the bathroom, I realized there were other people in the flat, and they were looking for me. I didn't know what instinct it was that told me they meant me no good. Perhaps, it was the frantic way in which they were knocking on the bathroom door. How long was it since we had consumed the drink? Not very long I suppose. Through the window of the bathroom, I could see the streetlights below and the moon in the sky. They must have immediately realized one body was missing – but they could not be sure if I was living or dead. I thought it would be best if they thought I was dead and I managed to escape through the window of the bathroom before they broke down the door and came for me.

Of course I wasn't thinking with such clarity at the time. It was all a jumbled-up instinct of self-preservation. I cannot clearly recall what happened after that.

Even as the banging on the door continued, I managed to squeeze myself out of the window and drop down on the pavement two floors below. It was a hard landing and I hurt my shoulder. But I did not care too much about it: my only thought was to put as much distance as possible between the house and me. There was no one on the road, at least none of the people looking for me. I think they did not realize that one of us could be alive. The night was warm, and I walked hurriedly down two blocks before I found a police patrol car. As I approached it, I saw the officer staring at me in shock. That's when I realized I was completely naked. The officer gave me his jacket.

The statement ended there, but Tim Taylor continued:

Armed with this statement, the police launched an investigation into Vasant Sena. Hope had taken the police officers to the flat where the bodies were found. There was, however, no sign of any intruder and it could never be confirmed if there were any body snatchers at all or if she had imagined it. She was a little bit off, a bit hysterical, a tad paranoid.

The post-mortem reports revealed that all of them had consumed a cyanide concoction mixed with orange juice.

'Hope as well?' I interrupted.

'Yes,' said Tim.

'So how did she survive?'

'According to medical reports, her body rejected the poison because the amount she had consumed was way more than what was necessary to kill her. Someone had fucked up the dosage.'

There was little proof, Tim continued, that those who had taken part in the mass suicide were even members of Vasant

Sena. Nevertheless, the police managed to convince a magistrate to give them a search warrant to raid Yogi Premananda's ashram.

What the police had not anticipated was the public relations shitstorm they were hurtling towards in their eagerness to solve what promised to be a high-profile case. They had not accounted for Yogi Premananda's influence and resourcefulness. He was a powerful man with friends in important places. The news of the raid was leaked to him. Consequently, when the police teams arrived at the gates of the ashram, they were welcomed by the Yogi and an entourage of camera-wielding journalists – including Tim. No one tried to stop the police from entering the ashram. On the contrary, the Yogi provided them with guides so that they could inspect every nook and cranny. The purpose, presumably, was to make all these armed men and their growling dogs look silly. The strategy succeeded gloriously because the police found nothing. There was no trace of any contraband, anything even remotely illegal, not even a scrap the police could have seized as evidence. Even as the hapless raid was on, the Yogi held a press conference at the gates of the ashram, using the full force of his considerable rhetorical skills – calling out the racism of the police and the administration. He accused them of targeting his peaceful organization because it was non-white and non-Christian. The men in uniform had no option but to leave, licking their wounds.

'So that's it?' I felt rather deflated.

'What do you think the police could have done without any evidence?'

Tim was right. But, he was yet to finish his story.

'You know, I am a hard-headed, old-school kind of journalist,' he said. 'So I took down all the information from my sources in the police and tracked Hope down.'

She lived alone in a tenement in the seedy part of Auckland. When Tim reached her flat, he was surprised to find no security, though she was in the police's witness protection programme. At first, she was suspicious, cagey, but Tim won her over by offering to buy her dinner. 'Oh man, could she eat. It was as if she had come out of Liberia,' Tim said. Only after she had polished off a full bucket of chicken, half a dozen pints of beer, and a double sundae, did she start to speak. What she described in lurid detail were the sex rituals at the ashram. There was, of course, no way to corroborate these claims, but they were juicy enough to make the cover of the features section, Tim thought. As Hope was very drunk, he dropped her home on his motorcycle.

The next morning, Tim was woken by a call from a police officer he knew.

'Did you sleep with her?' the officer demanded.

'Of course not.' Tim was outraged and explained about his story.

'I suggest you hold the story for now,' the officer told him. 'Hope was murdered last night.'

'What? How?' I heard myself screaming.

'Yes, I thought that would interest you.' Tim came so close to me that I could smell the tobacco on his breath: 'Her heart was surgically removed while she was still alive.'

SIXTEEN

When your eyes have been opened to something, you cannot shut them again and pretend to be oblivious to it. That is what happened to ACP Ashutosh after the meeting with Muzammil. Was he unaware of the activities of Vasant Sena till then? That seems quite unlikely. Yet, at the same time, what reason had he to be overtly interested in this religious organization? They had given neither him nor the rest of the police department any cause for curiosity, and in this relative obscurity, they had grown and flourished. Perhaps, this was a premeditated strategy: to remain subterranean, below the radar of surveillance, till their numbers had multiplied and their organization had expanded, sprouting innumerable branches, somewhat like the underground sewage system in the city.

Ashutosh knew there were no maps or blueprint for the network of drains beneath the streets. Much of it, especially in the older, northern parts of the city, had been constructed in the nineteenth century, and all the official documents related to this had been destroyed in a fire that gutted a wing of the Calcutta Municipal Corporation building on S. N. Banerjee Road a few years ago. Now, the army of human scavengers that the civic body employed to clean the drains would descend into the sewage catacombs like Victorian archaeologists exploring the legendary mines of a Biblical monarch. Among them, rumours of underground monsters and prehistoric demons were in wide currency, reinforced by frequent accidental deaths in their ranks.

The ACP was unaware of all this, and even if he knew it, he would not have cared too much…at least, not right then. But Ashutosh had an uneasy feeling in his stomach, a gnawing suspicion that, undetected by anyone, the Vasant Sena had grown into a dark, diabolical enterprise. He decided to investigate their activities.

But where would he begin?

Rukmini, he thought, getting behind the wheels of his car. Her in-laws had a close association with the Sena. She would be the perfect source, a most convenient point of entry.

He was supposed to go to her home that night for dinner. This of course also meant everything else afterwards, and the very thought of it filled him with eager anticipation. Rukmini was an epicurean in the realm of *eros*, vested with considerable imagination, allowing her to transform every encounter they had into an unforgettable performance. It was not uncommon for Dr Bose to be out of town at least four or five days a month, and when the opportunity presented itself, there would invariably be an invitation from her.

Ashutosh looked at his wristwatch. It was 6.30 p.m. Before he could go and meet Rukmini, he had two other engagements related to the murder of the girls. He turned on the ignition of the car.

His first destination was the house of Anasuya Chatterjee, the twelve-year-old student of Welland Gouldsmith School, whose body was found in a garbage dump on Ballygunge Circular Road. The Chatterjee family lived in a new multi-storeyed building behind Prachi cinema. Driving out of Tiljala, Ashutosh took Darga Road, straight on to CIT Road. This was the shortest route to Moulali. The drive would hardly take him thirty minutes, during which he tried to recollect all he knew about the family.

Anasuya's father Asim Chatterjee was a senior executive with Naxalbari Tea Gardens, which had estates not only in Darjeeling but also in Assam. Asim began his career at the company as a junior marketing executive but had scaled the hierarchy swiftly, by carving out a market for the company's first flush tea in the German Democratic Republic. This required him to spend three months in East Berlin every year; the company also sponsored his family holidays in Prague and Vienna and had given him a three-bedroom flat and a chauffeur-driven car – perks to retain him.

His wife, Asima, was five years younger than him, and taught Bengali at a government college in north Calcutta. Her career, however, seemed to have ended with the death of her daughter. It was more than three months since Anasuya's death, but she had not returned to teach. Asim had rejoined work within a week of the last rites.

Ashutosh had no problem in finding parking or entering the building complex where the Chatterjees lived. On seeing his police ID card, a security guard even volunteered to escort him to the lift and direct him to the right flat. But, as he stood in front of the thick wooden door, Ashutosh hesitated for a moment. He knew that his *suo motu* investigation was not strictly within accepted police procedure and conducting this informal interrogation with Asim would hardly be as easy as it was with Dashrath Manjhi. He did not have the authority to compel them to cooperate; they could demand the presence of a lawyer, report him to his seniors, or flatly refuse to meet him, and that would be it.

Asim Chatterjee answered the door himself. Unlike the security guards, he was not in the least impressed with the ACP's ID card; instead he was irritated.

'What's this about?' he asked, without inviting Ashutosh into the flat.

Even as he narrated the well-rehearsed spiel, Ashutosh noted how tall Asim was. The ACP himself was six feet; Asim would easily have been a few inches taller. This was unusual in Bengali men and it imparted a strange gravity to him. Ashutosh also noted how Asim's lips were permanently curved downwards, in an expression of acute irritation. It was not as if something displeased him, he was displeased because he felt entitled to it. This was a sort of entitlement that one associated with class and authority.

'I thought the police had already arrested the murderer,' he said after hearing out Ashutosh. 'At least that's what the papers are reporting.'

'Yes,' replied Ashutosh, 'but we thought the investigation should continue.'

'Why?'

It was a rare person who could make the ACP uneasy. 'We need to ensure that we have not missed anything,' he said. 'Is it okay if I ask you a few questions?'

Asim backed away from the door and indicated that Ashutosh should enter the flat.

'You should have called before coming,' he said. 'My wife is very unwell, and your visit will upset her.'

'I'm sorry Mr Chatterjee. I understand...'

'No, you don't.'

They were in a short, narrow corridor leading to the drawing room. Asim was ahead of Ashutosh, but he turned around suddenly.

'I'm sorry?' said Ashutosh.

'Please don't keep repeating that. You understand nothing. Do you even have children?'

Ashutosh felt an intense desire to punch the man across his jaw, to pluck out his eyes, to tear off his tongue. Yes, he did not have a child, but what did this man know about how much he wanted to have one, and why he could not.

'No,' he said.

'Then how can you even begin to understand the state we are in?'

Asim turned around and walked into the drawing room. Ashutosh stood rooted to the spot, stunned. He knew that he could not afford to succumb to the anger that was making it difficult for him to breathe and his palate was as dry as wood. With great effort he swallowed the fury and followed Asim.

The first thing he encountered in the room was a shrine to Yogi Premananda. It was a near replica of the one he had seen in Rukmini's house, only larger and more ostentatious, with a string of coloured light bulbs strung around it. These blinked on and off rhythmically. In the otherwise tastefully decorated room, the shrine looked completely incongruous.

Ashutosh looked around: the drawing room was large and sunny, though it was already late dusk, and the sunlight was fading very quickly. The large French windows opened towards the south, into a large balcony. These were pulled back and the smell of a *cadamba* tree nearby filled the room. There was hardly any furniture except a wooden sofa set in the middle of the room. It was not a new piece; in fact, it was unfashionably old and had possibly been in the family for a few generations. Though there was enough natural light in the room, the tubelight was on.

Asim occupied a single sofa and indicated with his hand that Ashutosh should sit opposite to him. Between them was a large, solid wooden coffee table, with a glass top.

'I see you are a member of Vasant Sena,' said the ACP.

This angered Asim even more. 'Are you here to talk about my daughter's murder or my religious beliefs?'

'I was only curious.'

'You see officer, I do not have the time to satiate your curiosity.'

Ashutosh looked at his subject. This was not a man accustomed to being contradicted, to have his wishes ignored. It was impossible to push him into anything. One needed guile and cunning to catch him on the wrong foot.

'Do you know Dr Sushovan Sengupta?' said Ashutosh.

'No,' replied Asim. 'Who's that?'

'He is the man we have arrested. Dr Sengupta is accused of killing your daughter – and the other girls.'

A strange expression came over Asim's face.

'What do you mean by asking me these questions? Why do you suppose I would know the killer of my daughter?'

'In my experience, most victims know their killers.'

'I don't give a damn about your experience.' Asim had not moved an inch, but it seemed to Ashutosh that he had grown. 'Do you not realize what kind of people we are? We are *bhadralok*. We have no connection with any criminal.'

'That's not what I am suggesting at all. I was only trying to do my job…'

'No, you are not,' Asim cut him off. 'All you are doing is harassing us. I think you should leave.'

Asim stood up and moved towards Ashutosh, as if he intended to throw the ACP out of the house. Ashutosh thought for a moment that he would be attacked, and his stomach coiled up. In his mind, he played out how he would destabilize and disable his adversary. He was taken aback by Asim's reaction to his rather polite questions. Even if one made an allowance for the grief of a bereaved parent, this was a bit much. It was also very disconcerting to see the layers of the bhadralok fall away and a bestiality emerge from the remains.

But even more disconcerting was the pair of eyes he found fixed on him from the far end of the room.

They belonged to a woman who had arrived unseen by them and was now standing near the door that led to the inside of the flat. She was partially concealed by the thick curtains on the door. The eyes did not look quite normal, their pupils seemed unnaturally dilated. The physical appearance of their owner was also a little strange, dishevelled. Her sari was tied loosely, and her hair fell in waves around her shoulders and chest. Even more strangely, though she did not look any older than forty or forty-five, every hair on her head was white. This last detail startled Ashutosh.

Following his gaze, Asim turned around and saw her. He screwed up his face in worry.

'Asima!' he said. 'Why have you come out?'

She did not answer the question. Instead, she asked, 'Who's this?'

Her voice was unnaturally low, but clear enough for the ACP to hear even though he was sitting a few feet away.

'Asima, don't stand there,' Asim said. 'Go inside.'

She showed no sign of having heard him. 'Who's that?' Asima repeated.

'No one.'

'Is he one of them?'

'No.'

Asim had started moving towards her. Seeing him approach, Asima gripped the curtains, resolved not to go inside.

'Tell me, is he one of them?'

It was a plaintive whisper, but it failed to move her husband. 'Did you have your medicines?' he said.

Asim was now standing right in front of her, as if challenging her to disobey him.

He repeated the question. 'No,' she replied.

'Go inside and take your medicines.' Every word he uttered was slow and deliberate.

Asima looked from him to Ashutosh, and for a moment it seemed that she might charge into the room. But then she lost her resolve and went inside.

Asim came back and sat down on the sofa.

'Was that Mrs Chatterjee?' asked Ashutosh.

But Asim was distracted, 'What did you say?'

'I was asking if that was your wife.'

'Yes, why?'

The ACP hesitated for a moment before asking if it would be possible to have a word with her.

'Out of the question. Did you not see what state she was in?'

'Is she not well?'

For the first time since they had met, Asim seemed to soften a little. 'She has not been herself since the death of our daughter,' he said.

Then, suddenly covering his face with his hands, Asim started to weep. Ashutosh was still wondering what to do when the room was plunged into darkness. It was a power cut. They had not noticed when dusk had sneaked up on them.

SEVENTEEN

Tim and I were also sitting in the darkness in the lobby of the hotel, drinking gin and tonic steadily. The drinking was a sort of contest: the Indian police officer could not appear to have lesser capacity than the Kiwi journalist, and vice versa. So, both of us kept getting more and more drunk. Our conversation stopped, started, picking up as our thoughts did and then trailing off again. Perhaps, both of us were also dozing off intermittently, lending a tattered, inconsistent quality to our conversation.

'Such things are common in places that have experienced civil strife,' he began at one point.

'What things?'

'Strange crimes – like the death of these girls.'

I did not quite understand, so Tim continued, 'Places, especially urban areas that have been the site of civil unrest often also become the theatres of crime such as the murder of these girls that we now have on our hands. It is a sort of collective psychological monstrosity, a by-product of the claustrophobia that citizens experience living constantly in the shadow of death.'

All this seemed obtuse to me, and I told him so.

'Let me give you an example. During World War II, the Nazis occupied Czechoslovakia and started using the resources of the country to manufacture munitions. Soon after, in Prague, there started circulating stories of Spring-Man Perak, a light-footed diabolical beast who could jump over buildings and leap across rivers. He lurked in the shadows of the city and painted anti-German graffiti high up on the walls of buildings.'

'That must have been the propaganda wing of the Czech resistance working overtime,' I said. 'What has it got to do with our case?'

Tim took a deep breath, like a teacher running out of patience. 'Let me give you another example,' he said. 'Have you heard of the Oil Man of Congo?'

I had not, so Tim explained.

'Right after the end of the civil war in Congo in 1965, there appeared a diabolical creature on the outskirts of Kinshasa, especially in the poorer areas. He was called Oil Man because he was covered all over with a viscous, black substance, possibly turpentine. He spread terror by attacking women, raping and killing them. He was never caught.'

'What are you trying to say?'

'I told you. Places that have experienced civil strife also often have such crimes.'

This theory seemed a little far-fetched to me. 'Even if we were to accept this hypothesis,' I said, 'what has that got to do with Calcutta? There has been no civil war here.'

The journalist looked at me as if I was completely stupid. 'How old are you?' he said.

'What?'

'How old are you?'

Though I did not understand what he was getting at, I told him my age.

'You are not too young to remember the Naxalites,' he said. Finally, I understood the circuitous route he had taken to make a rather simple point. Though what relation the Naxalite movement had to do with the current crimes I could not understand.

Tim continued, 'I've heard it was visceral. There were apparently entire areas in the city completely occupied by the guerillas. They were targeting and assassinating policemen and their informers. The retribution of the state was also quite brutal, entirely out of proportion. It wasn't uncommon in those days to find bodies of young men – real or suspected Naxalites – on the streets, murdered by the police or political goons.'

He did not need to tell me about those days, I remembered them more than I wanted to. 'Mr Taylor,' I said, cutting him off, 'you are still not making much sense.'

Tim poured another round of drinks.

'Guess who was a Naxalite as a young man,' he said, smiling.

'Who?'

'Yogi Premananda.'

This time, I was dumbfounded. Tim was obviously enjoying the dramatic effect his revelation had produced.

'You can't be serious,' I said.

Tim took out another piece of paper from his bulging folder. 'In September 1971, he was arrested for subversive activities,' he said. 'This is a copy of the FIR.'

I read the paper. It mentioned the relevant sections of the Indian Penal Code. But, the name of the accused was different: Arindam Chatterjee.

When I pointed out this incongruency to Tim, he laughed. 'Do you think he was born as Yogi Premananda?'

Before turning to religion, the Yogi had a different name and a different identity. At the time of his arrest, he was a young professor of chemistry at the Rajabazaar Science College. His colleagues and comrades from the time claim that he had transformed the chemistry laboratory of the college into a workshop to manufacture bombs for the Naxalites.

'He was particularly good at making Molotov cocktails,' Tim added.

Professor Chatterjee was also a firebrand ideologue, distributing Mao's *Red Book* and Marighella's *Minimanual* among his students.

'How did you find out all this?' I said.

'You surely can't expect me to reveal the names of my sources to you,' Tim replied.

During my conversation with Tim, I had realized that it was impossible to make him answer questions that he did not want to. So I posed a different one: 'What happened after the arrest?'

'Who knows what happened to him in the lock up? Calcutta Police have a reputation for being rather persuasive interrogators, don't you? Once you get your hands on a person, you can make them dance to your tune. If they don't, they might not come out of your custody with their body and soul together…'

Tim went on enumerating all the human rights abuses we have been accused of. What would he know to what extent one needed to go in pursuit of truth?

Also, I thought I should call Ashutosh immediately. My boss, I was sure, would consider my mission that day a success, with all the information I had managed to gather. Even if Tim did not tell me the names of his sources, we could confirm the details from our records. Perhaps Ashutosh had also found out things through the day that he needed to tell me.

I recalled that I was supposed to meet him at Rowdon Street. I had completely forgotten about this.

'Where is the telephone?' I said, hurriedly getting up from my chair, but falling back almost immediately.

The liquor had gone to my head and the garden and the portico were swimming in front of my eyes.

'Are you okay?' Tim sounded worried, also very far away.

'Yes, yes, I need to go,' I said.

But I did not feel I had the strength to get out of the chair.

Two thoughts were hammering on the walls of my brain: I needed to call or meet Ashutosh immediately, and I also needed to urinate urgently.

'Where is the bathroom?' I said.

Though time and space were not very distinct in my head, I could tell that Tim took a longer pause than necessary before answering: 'You can use the one in my room.'

His voice was incredibly kind, and his strong hands held me and lifted me from the chair. I don't think I could have negotiated my way to the bathroom, leave alone Tim's room, which was on the first floor of the building. He put one arm around my waist; with the other, he held the thick wooden balustrade of the yawning staircase. My left arm was around his shoulder. With our bodies fused together like this, we started travelling up the stairs. From my perspective, we might as well have been in a watery dream. The stairs looked like those in unclear pictures of sunken ships. They were fluid under my feet. I think I slipped a few times, but Tim's arms held me steadily. I don't know how he kept a clear head because he must have also been quite drunk. Perhaps it was his relative familiarity with the space, or perhaps he had more capacity for liquor than I did. Tim later told me that he counted every step as he mounted the staircase.

Having finished my business in the toilet, I returned to Tim's room and sat down on his bed. Well, not so much as sat down as fell down. I did not have much control over my limbs and motions.

'Here, have this,' said Tim, giving me a glass of water.

The room was modest by any measure. The furniture comprised a bed, made double by joining two singles; a writing table; two chairs; and a dressing unit. A cupboard was built into the wall. The floor was covered with a dirty green carpet. On one side of the bed, there was a small pile of clothes, newly washed and smelling clean.

Returning the glass to Tim, I said: 'I need to go. Can we call a taxi?'

'You won't be able to go,' he said.

'Why not?'

'Look, there's a storm.'

The room did not have any windows – the only source of ventilation was a door that led to a small balcony. It was open, allowing a glimpse of the sky. Everything was awfully dark outside as the clouds had covered the moon and all the stars. A steady, abrasive wind was playing foul with the trees.

Tim decided to go out into the balcony; I followed him. The air was wet.

We stood in silence for a few minutes, looking out at the rooftops of buildings, as the wind grew wilder like a rabid mongrel. It picked up fists full of dust and flung it in our faces. We could taste the sand on our lips.

Without any warning, Tim turned his face towards me and put his mouth on mine. His strong hands held the small of my back and pressed our bodies together, closer than on the drunken stairs. Instead of recoiling, I reciprocated, returning the force, the playfulness of his tongue with mine.

It was like diving into a deep, deep pool. When we came up for air, I asked him, 'How did you know?'

He smiled and replied: 'Don't we always know?'

'Is that why you got me drunk?'

'What do you think?'

There was thunder and lightning, and the rain obliterated the nightmare city like a great deluge.

EIGHTEEN

The mansion stood at the corner plot on the intersection of Rowdon Street and Theatre Road. ACP Ashutosh had parked his car on the opposite side of the road. Sitting behind the steering wheel, he was smoking and keeping a watch on the house, I was supposed to meet him around 7.30 p.m., but as I had not arrived, he was waiting for me.

The area was shrouded in darkness because of a power cut, but all the windows of the mansion were lit up. Even from a distance, the ACP could hear the constant gunning of a diesel-run power generator that was the possible source of illumination. Though it made quite a racket, intruding into the silence of the evening, Ashutosh was thankful for it as the light allowed him a better view of the property. It was enclosed by an eight-foot-high boundary wall and there were lots of trees on the grounds. The building itself was constructed seventy to eighty years ago and looked a little like a castle, with turret-like structures at its four corners and the roof a little like the ramparts of a fort.

With considerable unease – but also a strange satisfaction – Ashutosh observed the familiar yellow flag of Vasant Sena flying from the rooftop of the mansion.

In this palatial house lived the family of Aanchal Agarwal, the ten-year-old girl whose murder had prompted Ashutosh to relaunch the investigation.

The ACP looked at his watch: 7.20 p.m. He expected me to arrive punctually. Lighting a cigarette, he started thinking of everything he knew about the family he was going to visit soon.

The Agarwals were one of the most prominent families in Calcutta. Their ancestors had arrived in the city in the middle of the nineteenth century, escaping a drought in Shekhawati. In the beginning, they traded in textiles and spices, but had soon diversified into foodgrain. During World War I, they started trading in coal and their wealth multiplied many times. The Agarwal Mansions came up on Amherst Street. It was a prominent addition to the palaces of north Calcutta, an architectural innovation, combining Greco-Roman pillars with *jharokas* from Rajputana. But along with prosperity came discord. The many cousins in the second and third generations decided that they could not continue to live and work together and carved up the wealth among themselves. The older, northern branch of the family, with its base in Amherst Street, decided to invest in cinema, made huge losses, and was forced to sell off all their property, including Agarwal Mansions. The ones who bought all this were their southern cousins, who had established their base at Rowdon Street. They had invested in tea estates in Darjeeling and continued to grow exponentially.

The current head of the family and the business was Harilal, Aanchal's father. The forty-year-old widower was known for his short temper and love of fast cars. When he was about twelve,

Harilal had been sent to Eton. He spent the next twenty years in the British Isles and Europe, studying and travelling. He met his wife, another Marwari from Calcutta, in Zurich, where she was in finishing school. The couple lived in Rome and Paris, mingling with artists and writers and filmmakers, and were the perfect picture of domestic bliss. Their house in Calais was always open for expatriate Indian painters. This dreamy existence came to an end when Harilal's wife died suddenly in childbirth. Her body was not brought back home for some reason, and this sparked speculations that he had gotten rid of her. Harilal was rumoured to have had a roving eye and had apparently taken a fancy to a prostitute in Amsterdam.

Ashutosh had heard other rumours about him as well. Harilal apparently smuggled cocaine into India through the border with Bangladesh at Petropol. The tycoon was also reportedly hooked to the white powder. But he was untouchable, close to both the CPM and the Congress.

The real reason why the ACP had stayed in the car was because he did not relish the idea of an encounter with Harilal alone. But, it was already 7.40 p.m., and the ACP knew that Harilal did not meet anyone after 8 p.m. There was still no sign of his deputy, that is, me. Ashutosh wondered where I was and cursed me under his breath. Then, he rolled up the window of his car, got out and locked the door. Crossing the road without any hurry, he reached the wrought iron gates of the property on which hung the sign: BEWARE OF DOGS!

Harilal Agarwal was a bulldog of a man. He sat behind an enormous teak desk in his office at the front of the house.

Ashutosh was escorted into his presence by a security guard. As the cavernous room was lit only by an orange table lamp, it took Ashutosh a few moments to adjust his eyes to the darkness.

He saw Harilal smoking a fat cigarette. On the table in front of him was a dispenser filled with whisky, a jug of water, and a bucket of ice, and at his foot, on an expensive rug, sat a Doberman. As Ashutosh entered, it raised its head and pricked up its ears.

Indicating with his hand that Ashutosh should occupy a chair in front of him, Harilal asked: 'Would you like a drink, officer?'

'No, thank you.'

'I hope you don't mind *me* drinking.'

'Not at all.'

The ACP, who prided himself on his fluency in Bengali, noticed how Harilal had no accent at all. If you did not look at him while he was speaking, you would not be able to tell that it was a non-native Bengali speaker.

'So, to what do I owe the pleasure of this visit?' Harilal said.

Ashutosh hesitated for a moment. 'This is regarding the death of your daughter,' he said.

The tycoon bent forward and fixed his eyes, through bifocal lenses, on Ashutosh.

'Why do you use that word officer?' he said. 'Death? Was it just another death? No, sir! It was a murder.'

'I'm sorry for your loss.'

'Don't be sorry. Catch my daughter's killer.'

'That's what we are trying to do.'

'The hell you are!'

Harilal's hand came crashing down on the table, upsetting the glass of whisky. The Doberman raised its head and barked, twice.

'Can you tell me what you have done?' he demanded. 'Don't you know who the killer is?'

'Do you?'

Harilal threw his head back impatiently. 'I've already told you who I think it is.'

The ACP knew what he meant. During the preliminary investigation, the bereaved father had named his business rival and property developer, Amanpreet Singh, as the suspect. The police had taken Singh into custody and interrogated him, but we had to let him go as there was no evidence against him.

Harilal continued, 'I'm a law-abiding citizen. My father was a freedom fighter who went to jail with Gandhiji. You must have done your homework, so you probably know all this. My operations are all compliant with the rules and regulations of this country. Though, as I'm sure you know, with my contacts, I could have cut a few corners, avoided paying a few unnecessary taxes. But that's not my policy.'

Ashutosh waited as Harilal poured himself another drink.

'Business is business, and family is family,' he said. 'The sardar has made the mistake of mixing the two. Now, he has to pay for it.'

The ACP was acutely uncomfortable with the implications of such statements, and he tried to dissuade Harilal from pursuing an extralegal course, reciting the spiel that police officers regurgitate on such occasions.

This seemed to enflame Harilal even more.

'Don't tell me all this,' he barked. 'There is a different law for everyone, and in Bengal, there is no law protecting Marwaris.

We must buy our security here. Marwaris are to Bengalis what Jews were to Germans.'

Harilal embarked on a rant, the subject of which was hardly new to Ashutosh. He railed against what he considered the unjustifiable bad reputation of Marwaris, the hate and envy directed at them. When he began, there was an ironic smile on his lips, but as he got more and more outraged, the smile faded away and his eyes turned red.

'You hate us for our prosperity, our success, our lack of cultural refinement, but consider this: who has bankrolled your culture, your progressive politics, the infrastructure of your city? Your politicians come to me with their begging bowls and then make speeches where they paint me a villain. I hate them, I hate the whole lot, you bloody Bengalis!'

The ACP felt the last barb was directed at him, and though there was no need to, he decided to correct Harilal's perception.

'I'm not a Bengali,' he said.

'Then?' The Marwari was still foaming at his mouth.

'I'm a Bihari.'

Harilal paused for a moment and laughed.

'Do you know the relation between Bengalis and Biharis?' he asked. 'It is the same as that between Jimmy and I!'

Harilal's hand reached for the Doberman's collar and the dog started licking his fingers. He laughed again, and his laughter echoed in the turrets of his mansion.

NINETEEN

By the time Ashutosh started for Rukmini's house, it had already begun pouring. The distance between Rowdon Street and New Alipore is no more than seven kilometres and he should have taken about thirty to forty minutes to cover it. But, the ACP drove slowly as most of the stretch was waterlogged. The downpour had coincided with the high tide of the Hooghly. He was worried that the water from the streets, which had turned into canals for all practical purposes, would seep into the engine of his car, and it would break down, leaving him stranded in this weather.

He was also worried about other things. For one, what had happened to me? Quite uncharacteristically, I had not turned up at all. What was the cause of this insubordination, he wondered. Though he kept cursing me, he stopped at a pharmacy at Kalighat that was still open and used their phone to call the police headquarters. The operator who answered the call kept him waiting and ran to our floor to find out if I was there. When he came back to the phone, he told Ashutosh what he already knew: I had gone out in the morning and had not returned yet. The ACP then dialled the number at my home.

The phone rang, but no one picked it up. Putting the handpiece back on the cradle, Ashutosh looked at his watch: 9:30 p.m. He decided that his deputy needed to be reprimanded for this vanishing act. Then he lit a cigarette and stared out at the rain in the nocturnal city. It was coming down like a wall of water, opaque, a white darkness.

Ashutosh felt very uneasy, and what added to his unease was the city-wide power cut that he imagined was pursuing him, stalking him. It had been a very long day, and also, very hot, so hot in fact that it was suffocating to breathe the air, and now, the rain must have tripped off a power grid somewhere, plunging large parts of the city into this darkness. Ashutosh was not really a man prone to imagining things; he was pragmatic and analytic. Yet that night, he thought of the darkness as a black, stealthy dog. The ACP was taken aback at his own thoughts, but there was no rational antidote for the acidic emotions gnawing away at his heart, aggravated by the darkness around him. For the first time in his decades-long career, Ashutosh felt unsure of what direction to take. The case had become a contest between atavism and civilization, between sanity and madness.

Rukmini was sitting on the sofa, her feet folded under her, a glass of whisky in her hand. A servant opened the door for Ashutosh and escorted him in. She then took permission from Rukmini and left for the night. The rain had paused but one could still see the crow's feet of lightning across distant skies.

'Do you want a drink?' Rukmini asked as he threw himself down on the sofa beside her.

'Sure,' he said.

'You look exhausted. What have you been up to?'

'Police work.'

She did not ask any more questions but made his drink the way she knew he liked it: two fingers of whisky, a little water, and two cubes of ice. Giving Ashutosh his drink, Rukmini went behind him and started massaging his shoulders. After a minute or two, when she felt the muscles relax between her fingers, she whispered in his ears: 'Tell me.'

He told her everything: about every person he had met, conversations he had had, information he managed to collect or that which eluded him. Ashutosh left out no detail, as it was also his way of recollecting and classifying everything.

'It feels like scratching the surface of a mirror,' said the ACP putting down his empty glass.

'What were you expecting?' said Rukmini.

'Well, you see, in such cases – I mean serial killings – there is usually a common factor, something linking the victims. There is usually a common thread running through the murders, revealing the motivations of the killers.'

'What do you mean?'

'Say, for instance, the killer is a pervert who likes to rape prepubescent girls with blonde hair. So, we have a profile of possible victims. We can start looking at the list of history sheeters: do we have any suspect on our list? That's how we narrow down the search.'

'But there are common factors in this case too,' Rukmini pointed out. 'All the victims are young girls. All of them have had their hearts cut out.'

Ashutosh got up and started pacing the room. 'Yes, but that's where the connections end,' he said. 'There are also so many questions.'

'Such as?'

'First, the doctor we have arrested. He is obviously not the killer, at least not the only one.'

'What?'

'He was in police custody when the last girl was murdered. He could not have killed her. That means his accomplices – or the actual murderer – is still out there.'

Rukmini seemed very uneasy at the implication of this. 'I didn't think of it like that,' she said. 'What are you going to do?'

'The thing to do,' said Ashutosh, 'is to catch the killers. To prevent them from killing another girl.'

'How are you going to do that?'

The ACP noticed a strange urgency in her voice. 'I thought I would find something if I met the families of the dead girls,' he said. 'Something to link them, something we have overlooked. But, they are all so different, so starkly disparate.'

Ashutosh paused to light a cigarette. 'You can understand that the daughter of migrant workers, someone like Kumkum Kumari, would be vulnerable. But what about the other girls? They were from rich families, protected, well-cared-for.'

'So, did you find anything?'

The ACP paused for a moment before answering. 'You know, I did,' he said.

'What?'

He lifted his hand, pointed at the opposite wall, and muttered: 'Him.'

Rukmini followed his hand and saw what he was pointing at: the shrine to Yogi Premananda.

'What do you mean?' She laughed, a little nervously.

'Believe it or not, every family I visited today are members of Yogi Premananda's cult.'

'What does that prove? Everyone is a member of the Yogi's cult.'

'That's the thing, isn't it?' said Ashutosh. 'It's like an epidemic.'

The dinner started with asparagus soup and brioche, followed by fillet of fish, braised in butter. The main course was meatloaf with cranberry jam. Rukmini claimed that she had made it all herself – she had learned European cooking from an Anglo-Indian woman who lived near Rippon Street – so Ashutosh could not really tell her that everything was bland. There was no dessert.

After eating, Ashutosh poured another round of drinks, and the two of them sat on the sofa, their bodies intertwined. The power supply was still off, and the candles were now burning low, elongating the shadows in the room.

He remembered his decision to find out more about the Vasant Sena and its guru, and it occurred to him that Rukmini, who was also a member of the cult, could be a good source of information. She, however, seemed disinclined to discuss the subject.

Instead, she put her mouth on his, and allowed him to taste the whisky on her breath. He did not respond to her overtures immediately and she was quick enough to perceive his reluctance.

'What's the matter?' she said, disengaging from him.

'Nothing,' he replied quickly.

This was not enough reassurance for her.

'Did I do something wrong?' she asked, looking into his eyes.

At that moment, she looked so unsure, so vulnerable that Ashutosh could not help pull her towards him.

She began to kiss him again, not on his mouth but his chest, and traced her way down his stomach and below, her dexterous hand undoing his belt, her ravenous mouth swallowing him whole, her tongue skilful on the underside of his shaft. Almost involuntarily, he felt himself growing hard.

Ashutosh closed his eyes and took a deep breath. When he opened them again after a minute, he found himself staring at the shrine of Yogi Premananda, the candle flames dancing in the dark glasses covering the Yogi's eyes.

A troubling thought sprouted in the ACP's mind: Who was watching whom? Who was it that was actually under surveillance?

TWENTY

The Yogi was tall and thin, so thin in fact that you could call him emaciated. His face was pinched and hungry, and there was something feline about his curved nose. He usually wore a saffron tunic, like all the godmen across the country who were demanding that a Mughal-era mosque in Ayodhya be torn down and a temple to Ram be constructed in its place. A few months back, the Yogi had publicly declared his support for the cause and had promised a few lakh rupees to build the temple. He had also extended an invitation to the political leader travelling from Ahmedabad to Ayodhya on a chariot, to come to Calcutta and stay at his ashram. But the West Bengal government, led by the Marxists, had denied the politician and his entourage permission to enter the state, in a bid to prevent a communal flare-up. The Yogi was now planning his own chariot procession in support of the Ram temple...

The first time I saw the Yogi, it was his dark glasses that had caught my attention. They made it difficult to determine the true colour of his eyes. He wore them at all hours, day and night, never appearing without them, at least in public. Though no one had the faintest clue about the motivation for this strange behaviour, there were many rumours in circulation: his eyesight had been compromised by an accident in his youth; that he was quite blind and you could see the entire universe if you looked into his hollow cornea; that there were black fires in there to burn your soul.

'It helps with surveillance,' said Tim. 'With these glasses, he can look at people without them knowing that he is looking at them. Keeps them on their toes.'

'Surely, he can't keep looking at everyone all the time,' I said.

'Of course not, and one doesn't need to,' said Tim. 'You should know this as a police officer. The idea of surveillance is not actually to keep looking at people, but to make them feel like they are being looked at. That keeps almost everyone in line.'

We were sitting in the police jeep. I had parked it at the seven-point crossing of Park Circus. We were waiting for the Vasant Sena procession that was headed this way.

Vasant Sena has been taking out the annual procession at least since 1977, when the ban on them was lifted. What? Yes, they were banned at the start of the Emergency. Anyway, over the years, as the support base of the Sena expanded, the size of the procession also grew. For the police, this was a worrying development as the Vasant Sena members had grown more and more troublesome with the increase in numbers. Every year on this date, hundreds of Sena fanatics, doped on devotion, would pour out on the streets, feeling entitled to their celebrations. Many would be armed with rods and sticks and tridents. All of them were happy to die for their guru. How were we expected to keep them in check? This was not a regular political rally where most people turned up for the boxes of biryani they would get after spending a few hours listening to vapid speeches by one politician or the other. Followers of Yogi Premananda were drunk on rapture. Their skirmishes with the police had grown more and more frequent over the years.

'You guys can do nothing about it,' said Tim.

'What do you mean?'

Tim lit a cigarette and stared out at the road. It was eerily empty. Over the static of my walkie-talkie, I could hear the cymbals and drumbeats of the approaching procession. It made me a little breathless; the muscles in my stomach contracted.

We had been sitting in the jeep, smoking one cigarette after another, for nearly two hours now. I had been assigned this duty by Ashutosh. He was initially very angry with me because of my disappearing act, but afterwards, when we compared notes, he had grown more and more excited. This was because something he seemed to have deduced on his own was also seemingly confirmed by the information I had managed to glean from Tim.

The Kiwi had come with me out of journalistic curiosity, and I was glad to have him. But now, he was making me impatient with his silence.

'Well?' I said.

'Your approach is all wrong.' Tim passed me his cigarette. 'You respond to violence with counter-violence. You think the constable's stick, if wielded effectively, can restore order in the streets.'

'It is mostly quite effective,' I said.

'Yes, but not in this case.'

I passed the cigarette back to him and waited for him to continue.

'The rule of the stick works very well when all parties are working within the limits of reason,' he said. 'It is reasonable to fear the stick and fall in line. But what if someone was outside reason?'

All this philosophising was very frustrating. 'We know all this,' I said. 'The Vasant Sena members – at least most of them – have no reason at all. They are crazy. What we try to do is beat some into them.'

Tim looked at me and smiled. 'But do you know what it is that drives them?'

'Madness?'

'Love! But it is the same thing.'

A sudden burst of trumpets over the walkie-talkie interrupted our conversation.

'What do you mean?' I said, after the noise had abated.

The journalist put his hand on my thigh. 'Love is difficult to discipline,' he said, 'you cannot beat it into reason.'

'You are telling me that love is madness?'

'Exactly.' Tim chucked the cigarette butt out of the jeep. 'If you respond to their madness with violence, everything will spin out of control.'

I was going to ask Tim to expand on this, but he didn't let me. 'Look, here they come,' he said, pointing to the procession that was now within our sight.

The first thing we saw was the chariot. It wasn't really a chariot but a medium-sized truck that had been refashioned and decorated to look like the ornamental and historically inaccurate chariots of the mythological heroes in Ramanand Sagar and B. R. Chopra TV epics. It had a large cardboard umbrella, a cardboard quiver full of cardboard arrows, and even a dozen cardboard horses, their front legs up in the air. The truck, however, was driven not by a horse but a trusted driver. He maintained a pace that was neither too fast nor too slow. As it came nearer, we saw the Yogi in the chariot. He was not wearing his usual saffron gown, but a red one, covering him from neck to toe. He also had a monk's cap of the same colour and a pair of maroon shades. Around his neck was a thick garland of red hibiscus. Premananda's hands were high above his head, as he greeted the onlookers, millions of whom appeared suddenly on the pavements, on balconies and rooftops to catch a glimpse of him. The relentless midday heat seemed to bother them very little, though most of them were probably hiding indoors or in the shade till now. As they saw the Yogi, the people cheered and cried his name, invoking him to bless them. If they had not been held back by the police barricades, some of them would have gladly jumped in front of his juggernaut.

On the chariot with him were his bodyguards, a gang of twenty six-feet-tall Caucasian women. They wore brown uniforms and carried automatic rifles. According to information we had managed to gather, all of them were supplied to Vasant Sena by a Soviet company that provided mercenary military services. Some of the Yogi's guards had also reportedly served in Afghanistan. At times, the chariot would go too far ahead and would be forced to wait for the mass of Vasant Sena devotees following it. While waiting, the Yogi would stand, arms crossed over his chest and an impatient look on his face. He was a man in a hurry to get somewhere but he also knew that there was no point in getting there alone.

Behind him was the riotous, tumultuous approach of the crowd. First came the musicians and the dancers, relentlessly beating their drums and cymbals and blowing their trumpets. They made no music, but a lot of disorienting, confounding noise, like the roar of a distant ocean. The dancers were hysterical and uncoordinated. Many among them were not Indians at all, but Europeans, hippies. The men were mostly bare-bodied, wearing only dhotis. The women had pleated their saris in a manner that allowed vigorous movement. I suspected that the vigour was fuelled, at least in part, by hallucinogens. The police escort with them could barely contain them or keep pace. Next came Yogi Premananda's private militia. According to intelligence reports, it was 20,000 strong, armed to the teeth with the latest weapons including automatic and semi-automatic assault rifles, sniper rifles, and revolvers. Their most invincible weapon, however, was an unwavering faith in their guru. On the day of the rally, they did not carry any arms, nor did they come out in full strength. About 500 of them – tall, well-built men in khaki uniforms – arranged according to rank, marched down the road in grim silence. The final column of the procession was a far less disciplined group. They carried firearms and were occasionally shooting in the air. The police escort bringing up the rear of the procession seemed to have little inclination to take any preventive action against them. They just hurried them along.

When the procession had passed, a strange silence descended on the streets. One could hear the ceremonial flags fluttering in the wind. A murder of crows had set up an orchestra from atop lampposts.

I put down my binoculars and found that Tim's hand was still on my thigh. It had only moved closer to my crotch.

'What are you doing?' I said.

'What?' Tim's face was the epitome of innocence.

'Remove your hand.'

The sternness in my voice was also playacting; I felt deep erotic stirrings within.

Tim did not obey my command. Instead, he said, 'Why? You don't like it?'

'You are crazy.'

'I think we have already established that love is crazy.'

'You love me?' My voice was dry, uncertain.

Bringing his face so close to mine that I could smell the tobacco on his breath, Tim Taylor said to me: 'No, it is the lust I feel for your uniform.'

'Get away from me.' I pushed his strong shoulders with my hands. He threw back his head of dirty blonde hair and laughed.

'You know what they are going to do with us if they find out?' I said.

'Who?'

'The police.'

'You are the police.'

'I mean my bosses.'

'What will they do?'

'I don't know. Throw us into jail for being perverts.'

'Perverts? That's a bit too much.'

'This is not New Zealand. It's illegal here.'

He smiled again; his hand returned to my thigh. 'Well, if they do lock us up, I hope it is solitary confinement – only you and me.'

'Shut up.'

'Do you know what I will do to you when we get back to the hotel? I'll use your handcuffs to restrain you to the bedpost and fuck you while you are still wearing that uniform.'

With that, he lit a cigarette, jumped off the jeep, and walked away at a brisk pace in the direction of the procession. I kept sitting behind the steering wheel, utterly, helplessly, breathless.

TWENTY-ONE

The sound of machine gun fire on Little Russel Street seemed incongruous to Tim Taylor. It came in two short bursts, the second round lasting marginally longer than the first. He could not immediately figure out its source and started looking around.

How do I know all this? Well, some of it is from police records on that day. The rest is informed deduction. There might be a few subtle differences, but this how it all probably happened.

This was the fashionable part of town, where it would be more common to hear the strains of jazz or cabaret wafting out, along with the smell of soy sauce and spring onions, from an air-conditioned Chinese restaurant on a sultry afternoon like this. As the names of the roads – Theatre Road, Camac Street, Rowdon Street, Lawdon Street, Wood Street – suggested, these were all parts of the old colonial city, constructed mostly in the nineteenth or the early twentieth century. Tim was not unfamiliar with the area, having walked through its streets for hours on lonely evenings when he was a newcomer to the city. He knew that in 1964, the municipal authorities had renamed Theatre Road as Shakespeare Sarani to commemorate the birth centenary of the Bard. Tim knew that if you took a right at Wood Street, you would reach Saturday Club, which was established in 1878 by British civilians and army men as an exclusively white institution but was now run by Indians. The longevity of some of these institutions often surprised him. Take for instance the Calcutta Nursing Home: it was established by one Miss Brown in 1918, was taken over by a Bengali army doctor in 1926, and continues as a medical establishment even today. Another example was the Waqf Estate of Shahjad Begum at 33 Theatre Road – a property always owned by Muslims. On the day of the Vasant Sena procession, the police had thrown a protective ring around it. About half a dozen constables, armed with bamboo sticks, were strolling in front of it. The senior ones were sitting on a few wooden chairs placed outside the iron gates of the estate and listening to cricket commentary on a portable transistor. Most Vasant Sena members passed by without even glancing at the property.

Tim stopped to take a few pictures. He knew these were good ones and he could sell them easily to the *Auckland Star*. The meteoric rise of Hindu fanaticism in India had started attracting the attention of the international press. Perhaps, once this case was sorted, he could plan a trip to Ayodhya.

The voice of Yogi Premananda suddenly filled the afternoon air:

> *Arise, awake, and pause not till the goal is reached. What is our goal? To make this land the land of the pure, the true Hindu land. The day this happens, the condition of Muslims in this country will be the same as the condition of Hindus in Pakistan. Then every minaret of every mosque will sing: Jai Shri Ram.*

His voice reverberated through the crowds. The loudspeakers came alive, as the Yogi began his speech.

Tim started walking faster towards Chowringhee. After a few minutes, he came to the Lord Sinha Road crossing, and recalled another colonial institution in the vicinity that had continued to exist without too many changes. This was the headquarters of the police intelligence bureau, still functioning out of its old premises on Elysium Row. Its address might have changed in the municipal records – as the road on which it stood had changed its name – but it continued to serve the same purpose as before. The British police used to hold and interrogate freedom fighters and revolutionaries in this building, now the CID grilled and tortured radical leftists and Naxalites there.

Tim wondered if Yogi Premananda had also been kept there. Was he hung upside down from the ceiling and burnt with cigarettes? Did they pour petrol into his anus? What did they do to his eyes? Tim had heard from his friends in the police that the intelligence bureau building had a few rooms that had been soundproofed so that the screams of those being interrogated could not be heard outside. The drunk police officer who had told him about the methods of intensive questioning had also bragged about the scientific process used to break down the most hardened criminal.

'Don't let them sleep, keep firing away at them the same questions, till they tire out and are so confused that they confess,' he had said. 'It's like a ritual.'

Tim wondered what ritual they had performed on Arindam Chatterjee to transform him into Yogi Premananda.

If a Muslim wants to become a Hindu, we will accept him with love. We will purify him with Ganga water, we will integrate him into our society. But if they kill one Hindu, we will kill…

'A hundred Muslims,' the crowd cried out as Tim was passing through.

Vasant Sena supporters were all over the place, swarming like locusts. This was the tail of the procession we had seen from the jeep. Tim imagined it to be the tail of a prehistoric monster that had woken up after centuries of sleep, with an enormous hunger, and unleashed its rage on the streets, leaving destruction in its wake.

At last Tim saw the boy, no more than nineteen or twenty years old, drunk, careless. He had climbed a low wooden platform, usually the kind used by traffic constables, carrying an old Enfield rifle. He was screaming at the top of his lungs and his finger happily massaged the trigger. But the gun did not fire, it was probably jammed or dysfunctional. Tim felt like laughing at the boy. Was most of Vasant Sena's weaponry as old and useless as this gun?

A large crowd, comprising mostly participants in the procession, had gathered around to watch. A few Vasant Sena volunteers formed a cordon around the shooter and were trying to prevent onlookers from getting too close. They were also trying to cajole him to disembark from his perch. In the meanwhile, Tim thought he could get a few good pictures. Going down on his knees, Tim was trying to find a good angle, something from below that would make his subject larger than life, when the boy with the gun spotted him. He stopped screaming and firing almost immediately, as if his drunkenness had reduced. The boy turned his weapon towards Tim, holding it as if he was about to shoot.

But, the boy did not shoot. He stood there, his legs slightly apart, knees a little bent, almost casual. As the muzzle of the gun turned towards him, Tim stood up, his heart racing and his arms becoming stiff. Now, he realized that the gunman did not intend to fire at him at all. Instead, he was only posing, Rambo-like. Somewhere in his liquor-addled brain, he had realized that he had attracted the attention of the press, and he was trying to get a few good pictures taken that might find their way to the front pages tomorrow.

Tim obliged him, got down on his knees and pointed the lens of his weapon at the shooter.

He was still shooting away merrily when he felt a hand on his shoulders. He looked back and saw a very tall man standing behind him. From his position on his knees, Tim felt the man looked even taller, almost a giant. The journalist realized that this was a senior officer of the Vasant Sena militia: there were three stars on the shoulder patch of his uniform.

'What do you think you are doing?' he asked Tim.

Tim stood up to face his interlocutor and found the man still towering above him.

'Press,' Tim said, showing his accreditation card.

'Show me your camera.'

This was not a request but an order. The man was accustomed to having his commands obeyed instantly.

'Why?' Tim demanded.

'Do you have permission to take pictures?'

'Why would I need permission?'

'Your pictures are unauthorized.'

The Vasant Sena officer made a move to grab the camera, but Tim was quicker on his feet. He had anticipated that something like this would happen and had worked out a possible escape plan in his head. Before the officer could make another move, Tim turned around and started walking away at a brisk pace.

His progress was not easy as he was trying to walk against the flow of the crowd. Tim kept looking back to see if he was being pursued, and sure enough the Vasant Sena officer was never too far behind. Was his pursuer only after the pictures he had taken? He did not think so. He had proof of something that the Vasant Sena did not want to go out into the international press. Tim was certain that if the gigantic man caught up with him, he would probably not hesitate to eliminate him. In any case, Tim did not want to find out what his intentions were. He tried to increase his speed to put as much distance as possible between him and his pursuer.

Fortunately, he knew the area very well. From Middleton Row, he took a sharp left into Harrington Street. This road housed the American Embassy. It had been renamed Ho Chi Minh Sarani by a Left-controlled municipal corporation during the Vietnam War. For a moment, Tim thought the embassy could provide him sanctuary and started hurrying towards it. This road was not too crowded and did not have too many cars either. Turning back, he did not see the gigantic man following him. So he slowed down a little and tried to recover his breath.

TWENTY-TWO

The trouble began a little after midday. My jeep was still parked at Park Circus. I was standing on the road and smoking when I heard the first report being broadcast over walkie-talkie. The officer on duty at the Entally police station was asking for reinforcements to quell a street fight at Noor Ali Lane. This was a tough demand to satisfy on the day of the Vasant Sena rally, as most of the police force was spread thin over the city. The shift in-charge at the Lalbazaar control room responded to the call by asking for a little time while he scrambled a team together. The minutes passed painfully slow and updates on the clash kept pouring in. At first, it was not clear who was fighting whom and over what. The initial presumption was that it was a gang war, a clash between petty criminals over the turf they controlled. Then we heard the news of shots being fired. It seemed that at least one of the groups had country-made pistols. The distressed constable whose job it was to provide updates started speculating that this must be a skirmish between Congress and CPI(M) workers. It was now a triangular contest, with both groups trying to keep the police out of it. When a team of fifteen to twenty policemen tried to enter the narrow lane that was the site of violence, it was pelted with bricks. One constable's helmet was dislodged and a brick landed on his head, knocking him out. The police were forced to withdraw after firing a few teargas shells.

About twenty minutes passed before two teams from the Park Circus and Theatre Road police stations could reach the site. We have observed quite often that the actual exertion of force is unnecessary to quell a mob – the presence of a large contingent of armed policemen is sufficient deterrent for troublemakers. In this case, however, the police had to shoot quite a few rounds of teargas shells and even fire in the air before the miscreants finally dispersed, disappearing into the narrow lanes. By then, four or five shops had been vandalised and gutted, a few cars parked on the road had been set on fire, and two men had been killed. Their bodies lay on the road, uncovered, waiting for an ambulance from Chittaranjan Hospital to take them away for post-mortem. After the interrogation of the residents of the area, a clearer picture emerged: A group of four or five young men, carrying the Vasant Sena flag, had turned up at Noor Ali Lane and demanded that an eatery selling beef be shut down. When the owner refused, they started shouting slogans abusing the Prophet and the troubles started.

My colleagues had just about regained control of the lanes near Entally when reports started coming in of similar disturbances in other parts of the city, such as Kidderpore, Anwar Shah Road, Park Circus, Zakaria Lane, etc. These are, as you know, Muslim-majority areas of the city. Some sociologists have described these as 'ghettos' and it is not too far from accurate. There are various reasons for the geographical concentration of

Calcutta's Muslim population in these pockets. A Muslim man cannot buy or rent a house anywhere in the city except in the specific areas designated to his community. Hindu landlords will never rent out their property to Muslim tenants. Even if a landlord wants to, the Hindu neighbours will protest, raise a stink, and even socially ostracise the landlord for being too liberal and breaking ranks. Usually, the discrimination is carried out in whispers. University-educated, Left-leaning, middle-class Bengalis do not like to acknowledge their prejudice, but how many of them would be willing to get their sons or daughters married to Muslims? This exclusionary practice extends even to high-rises in south Calcutta. When Hindu flat owners of a building learn that the property developer is planning to sell one of the flats to a Muslim, they quietly get together and inform him about their concerns, thus nipping all possibility of 'pollution' in the bud.

The other reason for this tendency to carve out a separate geography is the insecurity with which most Muslims live in Indian cities. Since Independence – and Partition – there have been numerous communal riots in urban centres of the country, especially in the north. Calcutta, despite its claims of being more cosmopolitan and secular, is no stranger to religious hatred. The '47 riots were one of the worst in the country; in '64, hundreds were killed in a flare-up after reports of Muslims killing Hindus in East Pakistan started circulating. These are only the major ones; minor skirmishes are a daily affair. Naturally, Muslims – most of whom trail Hindus in almost all socio-economic parameters – find security in numbers and seek residence in areas where there are more of them. This has another repercussion. These areas are often viewed as concentrations of criminally inclined and communally-charged activities. The civic authorities and those in charge of law and order – that is, us, the police – remain apathetic to the needs of these 'ghettos'.

This concentration also makes them very easy targets, as we were to find out that day.

The early reports were patchy, unclear. We were not sure of what exactly was happening, though the walkie-talkie kept buzzing with news of trouble. A pitched street battle was in progress at Kidderpore. Some houses of Bihari coolies near the docks had been attacked and set on fire. In retaliation, the coolies blocked the western end of James Long Sarani, holding up trucks going out of town. When the police tried to remove the blockade, the protestors started throwing bricks, stones and cola bottles at them. The force was not strong enough to get things under control. Realising this quickly, the mob had become even more unruly and had set two or three trucks on fire. When a fire tender arrived from Behala to douse the flames, they stopped it as well and forced it to retreat.

It was not immediately obvious as to who was orchestrating these riots. Was it one group or many? Was it planned or spontaneous? What was the motive behind all this? Even as we were grappling with these questions, it became obvious that the police, spread thin over the city, was in no position to rein in the miscreants. The headquarters had asked for a few battalions of the Central Reserve Police Force, but it takes a little time for a central paramilitary force to be assigned. In the meanwhile, the situation was spiralling very fast into anarchy. It was like the outbreak of a disease – or madness. No one knew where it would spread next.

At the mosque on Zakaria Lane, the maulvi arrived for afternoon prayers and found a suspicious sack on the steps leading to the front entrance. It was stinking and oozing blood. At first, the maulvi thought it was a human body, but when the sack was opened, there could be no doubt that it was a pig. The animal has been gutted with an iron rod through its anus. The snout was intact, and the eyes were open. Two or three boys from the madrasa attached to the mosque ran to the Manicktala police station. The officer in charge would have rushed to the mosque but he could not. A large, belligerent crowd had laid siege to the police station demanding immediate arrest of the miscreants who had polluted the mosque. The more violent elements in the crowd said they would not allow the policemen to get out unless some arrests were made. Can you imagine the predicament? The patience of the mob was running low. They started pelting the station with stones and bricks, forcing the personnel on duty to barricade themselves inside and call for reinforcements. A team was hurriedly scrambled together and sent from the Shyamapukur police station. They had to engage in a three-hour-long skirmish with the mob and sustain a few casualties before lifting the siege and rescuing their colleagues.

TWENTY-THREE

I was following the developments closely over the walkie-talkie when another broadcast made my heart sink. The radio operator at the Park Street police station was informing everyone that a hotel on Sudder Street had caught fire. This was the same hotel where Tim Taylor lived. A small police team and a fire tender from Free School Street had been dispatched to the site.

As soon as I heard this, I turned on the ignition of the jeep and started for the hotel.

Perhaps I was not thinking straight but for some inexplicable reason, I took Theatre Road. This was the longer route. The Vasant Sena procession had gone down this road barely half an hour ago and the thoroughfare bore every sign of the wanton, rapacious vandalism that Yogi Premananda's devotees had unleashed.

This was one of the better roads of the city, unsurprisingly constructed by the British, like almost every good thing in Calcutta. Keeping it clean and not letting it to fall into ruin was a sort of validation for the otherwise dysfunctional municipal corporation. But as I drove down the road that day, it looked as if it had been hit by a hurricane. Every tree had its branches broken, cut off without reason and strewn about. The bulbs of almost all the street lamps had been smashed. To what diabolical purpose? I wondered. The entire area would be plunged into darkness at sundown as there was not enough time for repairs. All the shops had their shutters down and with good reason. One that had forgotten had suffered. It was a clothes showroom with display windows facing the street. The glass on the windows was gone, its shards scattered on the road. Even the mannequins had been dragged out and set on fire. Two had burnt down completely, their ashes being blown about by the wind. The third one had not been set alight properly. It was still standing, blackened by the fire, tongues of flames shimmering around its shoulders.

I stopped the jeep and stared at it for a moment. It could have been a man. The thought disturbed me considerably and, restarting the jeep, I sped off towards the hotel.

By the time I arrived at Sudder Street, the police and the fire officers had set up a perimeter around the hotel. Beyond it, you could see huge columns of smoke billowing out of one side of the building. I thought of all the woodwork inside the hotel: the broad staircase, the beams on the ceiling, the floors, windows and doors, to say nothing of the ancient furniture with which the place was cluttered. All this could keep feeding a small flame, transforming it into an inferno. Strangely, there was no fire truck around. There seemed to be no effort on at all to douse the flames still raging in the building.

I spotted a sub-inspector standing just outside the periphery and talking animatedly into his walkie-talkie. He did not see me come up behind him.

'What's going on?' I demanded.

He turned around, his face screwed into the officious irritation so familiar to all of us. 'Who the fuck are you?' he said.

I showed him my ID card. His demeanour changed immediately, and he saluted me.

'Where is the fire truck?' I said.

'It ran out of water, so it has gone back, sir. Another one is on its way.'

'What is the status of the rescue operation? Has the building been evacuated?'

He hesitated before answering: 'We are not really sure.'

'What do you mean?'

'There might still be one person inside.'

The sheer incompetence on display was very frustrating to me. 'How can you not know if a person is stuck inside?' I said.

The sub-inspector explained: all the staff members had been evacuated. They were standing at a distance, along with a small crowd that had gathered there, gawking at the spectacle of the burning building. 'The hotel apparently had only one guest,' he added, 'a foreigner, some sort of journalist.' Tim Taylor had apparently returned to the hotel about half an hour back, but the staff was not sure if he had gone out again.

'How can they not be sure?' I was starting to feel quite desperate now.

The sub-inspector was trying to explain something, but I cut him off. 'We need to put together a rescue team,' I said.

'Sir, we are not even sure if he is inside,' he said. 'He has not answered any calls.'

'Shut up,' I barked at him and hurried towards a group of fire officers who were standing a few feet away.

All of them were casually smoking. Even as I arrived, one of them finished a funny joke and the group erupted in uproarious laughter.

'What's going on here?' I said, interrupting them as rudely as I could. 'There's a man stuck inside, and you are standing here and laughing?'

The senior-most fire officer looked at me with an expression of absolute disdain. 'Who told you there was someone inside the building?' he said. 'We don't have confirmation on that.'

'You won't have any confirmation if you keep standing here and laughing,' I said, 'instead of going inside and finding out.'

'I don't think you understand.' The fire officer's voice was irritatingly calm. 'This is a very old building. We don't have any maps, we don't know how much damage the fire might have done. I'm not sending my men in to save someone who might not even be there.'

Then he said something that tore apart all my pretence at calmness: 'Even if someone were inside, he's probably dead by now.'

Without waiting another moment, I jumped over the jute rope that formed the perimeter and ran towards the hotel building across the dirty lawn. My actions must have taken everyone by surprise. I could hear them calling out to me, asking me to come back. By the time I reached the portico where Tim and I had sat drinking a few evenings before, the voices had faded behind me.

The ground floor of the hotel was thick with smoke, compelling me to cover my nose with a handkerchief. Before entering the building, I called out Tim's name a few times, but there was no response. One part of my brain was telling me that he was not even in the hotel and I should not venture into it. Yet, how could I just walk away without ensuring that he was safe? So, suppressing the claustrophobia I was already experiencing, I stepped inside the building.

It was like walking into a dark, subterranean pool. The smoke swallowed me, and I was lost to the world. There was hardly any light, making it nearly impossible to figure my way around. The smoke made my eyes water, adding another challenge to my expedition. The handkerchief was quite an ineffective precaution, and no sooner had I entered the smoke than I started coughing violently. But I pressed onward, trying to recollect the layout of the floor from memory and make my way to the staircase. I don't know how long it took me to reach it because I had lost all sense of time and space. Finally, I found the balustrade within the reach of my extended hand and started mounting the stairs cautiously. I was calling out Tim's name continuously though I could hardly hear my own choked voice. My feet counted every step I climbed, performing the task of my eyes, which had been rendered impotent by the smoke. I feared that even a small misstep would send me hurtling down and result in a fatal accident, but I somehow managed to reach the first floor without mishap.

I was not sure if Tim's room was on this floor. The last time I climbed these stairs, it was with his assistance and in a state of complete inebriation. I started trying to open the doors to every room. Most of them were locked, denying me entry. Though this floor was also almost completely in the dark, there was less smoke here, making it easier to carry out my search.

Almost at the end of the corridor was a door slightly ajar. I had not seen it at first, but when I finally did, I hurried towards it. Smoke was billowing out through the cavity of the un-shut door. This was accompanied by an acrid odour. Now that I think back on it, I wonder how I had not detected it as soon as I entered the building, or at least when I reached the first floor.

As I kicked open the door, the source of the odour revealed itself. Tim Taylor was sitting in the middle of the room, bound to a chair. But he was not moving. His body was aflame – exactly like the mannequin I had seen on Theatre Road barely an hour ago. His malefactors had constrained him and set him on fire. They must have poured enough fuel to keep the flames alive till now. Tim's fair skin had turned completely black with patches of red. The sight hit me like a wall I had slammed into. I lost consciousness and collapsed.

TWENTY-FOUR

Death is ubiquitous but ultimately meaningless, even inconvenient. When I came around, I found myself on a narrow iron bed in the general ward of Calcutta Medical College and Hospital. The ward was in a large hall on the second floor of the enormous nineteenth-century Greco-Roman edifice. This was the first temple to modern medicine in this country. The ward where I regained consciousness would have easily had a hundred beds or so, arranged in two long lines along its length. The western wall of the ward was punctuated at regular intervals by full-length French windows. These were always kept open, letting in a flood of sunlight. From my bed, I could hear the din of voices in the College Street market below, the sound of buses and trams.

The first thing I saw on opening my eyes was the ancient, languidly rotating fan on the high ceiling right above my bed. My bed clothes were completely drenched in sweat and the back of my throat was as parched as wood.

The nurses and orderlies were nowhere to be seen, so I decided to find water myself. As I tried to sit up, I found my head to be too heavy, wobbly. I had to hold on to the side of my bed to steady myself. Also, I was wearing only a loose-fitting gown and no underwear. It would be difficult to walk around like this without offending someone. Thankfully, the gown had a belt and I used this to fasten my clothes tightly around my waist. I did not have slippers either and was forced to walk around barefoot on the dirty floor.

No water was to be found in the ward itself. Most of the patients were asleep at this hour. Those who were awake looked at me though dull, glassy eyes. There was no one around who could help me, or for that matter, stop me. If I had wanted, I could have walked straight out of the hospital. Remembering all this, I am surprised that then my only thought was for water. I did not wonder even for once what had happened to Tim.

In the corridor outside, I found a row of taps protruding from the wall like a line of penises. I did not find a glass, so putting my mouth to the mouth of a tap, I started drinking.

Almost immediately, everything came back to me. It was as if the blood in my brain had clotted or the foundations of the building had grown so weak that the roof was collapsing on our heads. My knees gave way under my weight and my body succumbed to gravity. I don't know how long I lay on the floor, unconscious, before a male nurse found me and took me back to my bed in a wheelchair.

'Why did you get out?' he asked in a rude voice. 'Why didn't you call any of us?'

'There was no one around,' I said feebly.

This mild complaint seemed to incense him. 'Are you a child?' he demanded. 'Why didn't you ring the bell?'

He pulled out a switch from under my pillow. It was attached to a wire. He tried it twice and each time a distant ringing could be heard. Another nurse, a woman, came running.

'What happened?' she asked.

Her colleague did not answer her but instructed me: 'Don't move from here. I will go and call the doctor.'

He went away muttering how patients always behaved in an irresponsible manner and it was the medical staff that was always blamed.

The nurse returned with a doctor in a few minutes, but the interval seemed like an eternity to me. Anguish surged through my blood vessels and a hundred thoughts ricocheted in my brain. What had happened to Tim Taylor? How did I land up at this hospital?

The answer to the second question was easy to find. On seeing me rush towards the burning hotel, the firemen and the police officer had put together a rescue team and followed me. They found me unconscious where I had fallen and rushed me to this hospital. All police personnel in need of medical attention were admitted here. The diagnosis for me was shock and mild asphyxiation, and I had been put on oxygen.

After examining my blood pressure and pulse, the doctor declared that everything was higher than normal and instructed the nurse to administer a dose of sedative. There were a thousand questions I wanted to ask, but suddenly, fatigue washed over me like a wave. I neither protested nor felt the pin prick of the needle that brought me obscurity and shut out the dazzling afternoon.

It was not as if I was unfamiliar with loss. When I was ten, my father died. He was a traffic police sergeant and was murdered in August 1971 by a gang of ultra-Left students who wanted his service revolver. Investigations would reveal that they had tracked him for more than a month, following him from our home to the traffic police headquarters, and then to whichever corner of town he was posted in for the day. On three nights of the week, he would go drinking with his friends. They apparently followed him there as well. One night, they cornered him in a blind lane and stabbed him repeatedly. My father was so drunk that he did not even put up a fight. For his assailants, it was all futile, because he was not even carrying the weapon they coveted. All of them were arrested within a month and died in police custody.

My mother and I were accorded the status of the wife and son of a martyr and were recipients of a surfeit of sympathy. In the days following my father's death, relatives, neighbours, his colleagues, all started crowding our two-roomed flat at the police quarters in Jadavpur. They would come bearing rajanigandha flowers and paper bags full of old fruit bought at a discount. They would sit at the formica-top table, drinking the tea my mother served them, pontificating about how she needed to be brave. When they departed, my mother would put the fruit away and keep the flowers in makeshift vases of water bottles. At one point, there was so much rajanigandha in the house that I could hardly breathe, and since then, I have associated the distinctive scent of the flower with death.

I don't know if anyone bought rajanigandha for Tim Taylor. I could not find out much and making too many inquiries would have been awkward. According to the post-mortem report, which I acquired surreptitiously, the cause of death was asphyxiation and third-degree burns. As there were no other injuries to the body, the death was classified as accidental. There was no mention of Tim being tied up or anything. The New Zealand high commission had taken charge of his remains and sent it back home.

The cause of fire, according to another enquiry, was a short circuit. The wiring in the hotel dated back to the beginning of the century and had never been replaced but only patched up when necessary. It was obviously not strong enough to bear the load of modern equipment such as air conditioners and geysers. Though there was no concrete evidence for any of it, the police report constructed the events as follows:

> *Tim Taylor had returned to the hotel in the afternoon and had gone to his room unseen by anyone. Since his body had been found in the room, it was presumed that he had gone there on his own. He had apparently turned on the AC, had a few drinks (the post-mortem found alcohol in his stomach), and fallen asleep. The fire had started undetected by anyone, and had spread quite rapidly, the flames feeding on the old wood of the furniture and the dry curtains and carpets. By the time Tim woke up, he must have inhaled a lot of the smoke and was therefore unable to escape the inferno. The fire gutted his room and destroyed all his belongings. Not a scrap of paper could be recovered.*

Of course, this was the most convenient way to explain why someone with such good health as Tim had not been able to escape, though the staff of the hotel was evacuated.

I stayed in the hospital for a few more days. No one came to see me, as I had no relatives or friends in the city. My recuperation period comprised phases of sedative-induced unconsciousness alternating with vegetative wakefulness. As I lay awake in my bed, staring at the fan on the ceiling, two disparate lines of thought troubled me. First, what exactly had happened to Tim? Why did he go back to the hotel from his assignment instead of coming to me? What bothered me more was that none of Tim's painstakingly collected material could be recovered. His camera, which he had been carrying on the day of the Vasant Sena procession, was also missing.

Second, where was Ashutosh and how far had he progressed with the investigation? If our hypothesis was correct, the killer would claim his next victim any day now. What could we do to prevent it? This last thought would make me agitated, but there was nothing I could do about it.

When the doctors deemed me fit enough, I checked out of the hospital and went home.

TWENTY-FIVE

For quite a few days after being discharged from the hospital, I did not return to duty. A strange kind of lethargy had infected my blood, making it very difficult for me to do anything at all. I would usually lie in bed till midnight, passing in and out of consciousness, trying to shut out all thought, letting the hours wash over me till it was impossible anymore to ignore my hunger. This would usually be around the time the municipal school in my neighbourhood would get off. The cacophony of children being liberated from the institution would make it difficult for me to indulge my inertia. Then I would perform my ablutions and boil two eggs for lunch.

Around this time, a strange restlessness would grip me, making me want to get out of the house. Putting on whatever shirt and trousers I could lay my hands on, I would lock the door of the flat and set out. My inevitable destination would be Chhota Bristol at Esplanade, but I often took a circuitous route, first in a bus to Mayo Road, and then on foot to Park Street. My sole attraction there was the shop that sold antiques. In the dirty glass windows of the shop, there were innumerable marble lamps. I liked to watch the staff turning them on as the long summer dusk slowly turned into evening. Eventually, I would find my way to the watering hole.

At the bar, I had a few acquaintances, drinking companions. In the true nature of such inebriated companionship, I did not know what most of them did, where they lived, or even their names. The two that I knew were Jagannath Mondal and Madan Karmakar. You could hardly have met two characters so contrary to each other. Their tastes in everything differed starkly: if Jagannath supported East Bengal, Madan was a Mohun Bagan fan; the former could give up his liver for hilsa and the latter could sacrifice his kidneys for prawns. Yet, despite all differences, the two were inseparable, at least while drinking. The only thing they agreed on was Old Monk. Jagannath was a deeply religious man who always wore yellow shirts with 'Ram' or 'Om' printed on them. There were usually several necklaces or chains around his neck, with lockets bearing pictures of Lokenath Baba, Ram Thakur, and other saints. He was in the habit of massaging his paunch with his left hand and letting out cries of 'Joy Ma!' to punctuate his nightlong drinking sessions. I don't think I ever found out what he did for a living, but he never seemed to lack in cash. From how cagey he was about disclosing its source, I guessed it was not clean. Madan, on the other hand, was an agent of Life Insurance Corporation of India, and often ran short of funds. He was happy to borrow but did not always pay back. True to expectations, he was a self-declared atheist. There was a rumour about him in common currency at the bar: Madan was a spy for CPI(M), informing the Party about those too critical of it. So, usually when he sat down at a table, the others would shut up. The only exception to this rule was Jagannath who took great pleasure in riling Madan. They would end up fighting every night, like an old married couple.

One night, the altercation started after Jagannath told us about this ascetic in Howrah who could bring the dead back to life.

Madan could not resist the temptation to respond: 'If you are right, my company would never have to give out money to any claimant.'

'What do you mean?' Jagannath said.

'You know, to claim life insurance, one has to actually die. But if this Baba can really bring people back to life, we shall hire him. Whenever we have a claim, we shall get him to resurrect the dead person. That way we will never have to pay out anything.'

Jagannath considered this for a minute. 'Are you joking with me?' he said.

'Not at all,' replied Madan with a serious face.

But he could not help breaking into laughter. Some of us at the table joined him.

Jagannath was not ready to take this lying down and cried out with some passion: 'You are a communist!'

Almost everyone at the table stopped laughing, but not Madan. 'What has that got to do with anything?' he said.

In a rather dramatic motion, Jagannath knocked back his drink and declared in the voice of a martyr: 'Laugh all you want, but when you actually see him perform the miracle, you will laugh on the other side of your face.'

So, it was decided that Jagannath would take Madan and me to see a performance of this ascetic. The resurrection act took place every night at the crematorium on the banks of the Hooghly. The performance usually started around ten. It was already past nine, so we decided to pay the bill and took a taxi to Babughat.

We could have crossed the river on one of the larger steamers or launches but Jagannath insisted that we take a country boat. Halfway across the river, we saw the first streak of lightning beyond the cantilever bridge. We could hear the constant traffic of trucks and trams and buses on it, but it all seemed very far away. Jagannath guided the boat to an obscure ghat. The crematorium was adjacent to it.

There was not much activity going on at the crematorium. We saw a few *doms* standing around and smoking near the municipal office that issued death certificates. The office was right next to the building that housed the electric incinerators. I knew from experience that the inside of the building would be stuffy and full of smoke. We did not go towards it, but started walking in the opposite direction, towards the traditional wooden pyres. It had started drizzling. Madan took out his handkerchief and tied it around his head to prevent his hair from getting wet. He was grumbling about the futility of this exercise. Jagannath insisted that what we would witness would be more than fair compensation for our troubles.

We saw the fire of the yagna from a distance. As we approached it, we saw a puja in progress near a small shrine dedicated to some obscure god represented by a large, smooth stone. The idol was smeared with vermillion and covered with marigold and hibiscus. Sitting in front of the fire, his legs crossed, was a man of indeterminate age, conducting the puja.

His torso was bare, and his face had a huge beard. The ascetic's eyes were closed, and he was muttering some mantra.

'That's him,' Jagannath told us.

A small crowd had gathered at the spot – mostly other ascetics, beggars and drug addicts. We joined them and started watching.

Madan, however, was getting impatient. After watching for a few minutes, he said in a loud voice, 'What are we waiting for?'

A few heads turned to look at us. The eyes were vacant. Jagannath looked at Madan with reproach written all over his face and told him to keep shut. 'We are waiting for a dead body to arrive,' he explained.

Madan laughed softly. 'How do you know one is coming?' he said.

'It always does.' Jagannath's declaration rang with the certainty of the devout.

Our wait continued for the better part of an hour. The drizzle was threatening to turn into a downpour and I was cursing myself for allowing them to drag me into this. I was convinced that nothing was going to happen and was looking for the first opportunity to get out.

The clock of a nearby church let us know that it was ten. Almost on cue, a funeral procession started to make its way towards us. It was not a large procession, barely half a dozen men carrying the bier, crying: 'Bolo Hari, Hari Bol!'

They were headed towards the building that housed electric incinerators and would have walked right past us. But the ascetic, in a stupor till now, seemed to rouse himself suddenly and called out: 'Who goes there?'

'We bear the body of a child,' said one of the men carrying the bier.

'Come here,' the ascetic called out.

'What do you want from us?'

'I want to see the face of the dead child.'

At this point I thought the patience of the bereaved would run out. At best, they would ignore the demands of this crazy man and carry on. I would not have been taken aback had they started abusing him or even attacked him.

What they did, however, took me completely by surprise. The procession turned around and came right up to where the ascetic was sitting. The corpse-bearers put the bier down where he could get a good look. Like the others in his audience, I, too, bent closer to get a better look. The girl could not have been older than twelve or thirteen. Her face was devoid of colour.

'What happened to her?' the ascetic demanded.

'Snake bite.'

'Was she an orphan?'

'No, she was my daughter.' The last statement was made by a bald, middle-aged man who came forward.

The man started explaining how the facilities at the government hospital were no good, how they had got late, and how they did not know what to do, but the ascetic cut him off.

'Why did you not bring her to me?' he said.

On hearing this, the bereaved father broke down and started howling. Falling on his knees, he grasped the feet of the ascetic and started crying: 'Bring her back! Please, bring her back.'

The ascetic remained unmoved by all this. At length, he said, 'You think it is easy to get them back?'

'I know you can,' the father moaned. 'Tell me what I need to do.'

'To get one life back,' he declared, 'you have to give up another.'

As realisation dawned on him, the bereaved father got up and wiped his eyes: 'I'm ready to give up my life for my daughter.'

The ascetic started laughing on hearing this. 'Not your life, fool,' he said, 'you have to sacrifice an animal.'

He pointed to a black goat tied not too far away and instructed the father to go fetch the animal. Then he produced a scimitar from under the mat on which he was sitting and ordered the father to kill the animal. Almost immediately, four members of the procession gripped the goat by its limbs and held it down. Startled, the animal began letting out plaintive cries. This did not deter the father of the dead girl. In one swift motion he raised the weapon above his head and brought it down in an arc, severing the animal's head from its body.

Blood and flesh splattered everywhere. The beheaded goat shivered a few times before going completely still.

By now the audience was completely mesmerised. No one moved or said anything but stood staring at the bizzare drama unfolding in front of us. Even a sceptic like Madan had been struck speechless. I felt the hair on my hand standing on end.

All this, however, was nothing compared to the next instruction.

'Cut out its heart and bring it to me,' he told the grieving father.

Now that I think of it, I was struck by how strange the situation was. How could anyone except a butcher or vet be so familiar with the anatomy of a goat? The father was extraordinarily fluent in cutting out the heart of the animal and presenting it to the holy man.

What the ascetic did next was beyond my wildest imagination. Receiving the heart of the goat in his left hand, he put it to his mouth and bit into it. Blood shot out from between his teeth like spit and some of it rolled down his beard.

A strange revulsion overcame me and I could not keep standing there anymore. Without attracting the attention of my companions, I slipped away. The drizzle had turned into a steady downpour and I hurried back to the ghat where we had landed. My progress was slow as the road was unfamiliar and also very dark. At least three or four times, I felt nausea wash over me and I was sure that I would throw up. But I managed to reach the riverbank without any untoward event. Though the clouds were quite thick, it was possible to see all the lights on the opposite bank. All of Calcutta seemed to be lit up, enlightened. But I would have to cross the Hooghly on this dark and tempestuous night to reach it. Glad to have escaped the horrific scene, I took a deep breath in relief, and immediately an overwhelming burst of nausea churned my insides. I fell on my knees and started vomiting. A steamer hooted, twice.

PART THREE

TWENTY-SIX

The nose of the taxi driver was deformed, as if it had not been set properly after a fracture. Afreen noticed it in the rear-view mirror and it filled her with ominous thoughts, like the grey clouds that had filled the sky.

'It was an accident,' said the driver, catching her eye. Then, almost as if reading her thoughts, he added: 'You don't have anything to worry about. This was long ago. I'm careful while driving these days.'

As if that could reassure her. What could he possibly know of the concerns that afflicted Afreen, haunted her, kept her awake at night? These did not include getting into an accident while being stuck for half an hour in a mile-long traffic snarl in central Calcutta.

'How much longer do you think we are going to be stuck here?' she said.

'If the traffic starts moving, we will reach in twenty minutes,' the driver replied.

'But when will it start moving?'

'How can I tell you? There is a procession blocking the road ahead.'

The driver kept his eyes on the road. He was drumming the steering wheel with his fingers and whistling a song Afreen did not know. She had presumed that the procession ahead was a political one, but then she caught a glimpse of the participants, all clad in saffron and yellow, singing and dancing enthusiastically to the music of a portable harmonium that one of them was carrying.

The group went past the right side of the taxi, making their way unhurriedly through the narrow spaces between the stalled cars. When they were gone, the driver rolled down his window and spat outside, following it with a curse. Though Afreen did not know the word, she realized that it was an obscenity from the way the driver ejaculated it.

'What's the matter?' she said.

'I'm sorry,' replied the driver, 'but I can't help myself when I see these idiots.'

'What do you mean? Who are these people?'

The driver made a noise that was half a laugh and half a sneer. 'Haven't you heard of Vasant Sena?' he said.

Afreen had heard about the new-fangled religious organization with its dynamic new leader who demanded that a mosque in Ayodhya be torn down to build a temple.

'Lunatics!' the driver continued. 'Do you know how many people died in the riots they started last month? They are waiting to start some big trouble.'

He spat out of the window again. 'None of this would have happened if Yogi Premananda had been killed.'

'What do you mean?'

'Don't you know? He was attacked a few years back but survived.'

The driver began to narrate how a gang of criminals, possibly in the pay of the ruling Communist Party, had tried to assassinate the Yogi a few years back.

Afreen was too tired to decipher the fabulous narrative of the taxi driver, being delivered in a strange dialect of Hindi, with Bengali words thrown in generously. She sighed and fell back into the uncomfortable leather seat of the black-and-yellow Ambassador taxi and stared out of the window.

Calcutta was turning out to be every bit the black hole that everyone back home had warned her it would be. The first time she saw it from the windows of her compartment in the Kalka Mail, Afreen was filled with a vague dread. How could she ever hope to find her husband here? According to a letter sent to her in Srinagar from his landlord in Calcutta, he had gone missing a week back. That's all the letter had said. She tried calling him at the number she had, but no one had picked up the phone. She had even tried to contact his friend in Calcutta, but to no avail. If someone wanted to be lost, they could not choose a better place than this, and she was a little suspicious that he had planned it after all. Forcing the fear and suspicion down her throat, she had got off the train and taken a taxi from the stand outside.

Now, stuck in this car, she rolled down the window to let in a breath of fresh air. It failed to improve her mood and she started thinking of the strange circumstances that had brought her to this city.

They make a desolation and call it peace. A few days before taking the bus to Kalka, Afreen had read this line in a poem published in the culture pages of the *Kashmir Monitor*. The rest of the poem had made no sense to her, but this line stuck in Afreen's thoughts, like the stain of saffron on white fabric. When did it all begin, she wondered. Was it when her husband got a letter from his friend Bhajan Kaul, inviting him to join his business in Calcutta? How long ago was that? Was it six months? No, seven. It was February: the ice on the slate roof was still thick and the boats on the Dal were selling carrots and turnips. The postman who had come to deliver the letter was wearing a blue raincoat. She had offered him tea but he had refused, returning down the road in front of their house on his cycle, his raincoat flying behind him like a flag. It is strange how people remember these trivial details, forgetting the more significant ones. For instance, Afreen did not remember what her husband had looked like when he was departing. This was possibly because she had been racked with worry all morning after discovering that one of the wheels of his suitcase was broken. She had unpacked the entire thing, taken it to a repair shop and got the wheel changed. On her way she had to cross Guphar Road and the army check post. The soldiers on duty were languid. They did not ask for her identity card before waving her through. Everything was languid that day, it was raining, cold.

But the rain in Calcutta was very different. It was hot on the skin, humid. 'Alien rain,' Afreen said to herself.

The taxi was still not moving, so she returned to her original question: when had it all begun? Afreen thought that it all – the long road to desolation and peace – began with the crazy idea to build a mosque inside a temple in Jammu. If someone had not cooked up this foolhardy plan, there would never have been any riots in Jammu. If there had been no riots in Jammu, there would not have been any retaliation in Anantnag, and a mob would not have burnt down Bhajan Kaul's antiques shop. It was February then too. The day was wet; the remains of the shop, the cinders, were, however, still smouldering when he reached it. Her husband had brought Bhajan home. They had been friends since school. Afreen had never seen a man more devastated than Bhajan Kaul in the days after he lost everything along with his shop. He had stayed with them a few days, hardly ever speaking, before going to Delhi, after selling his house and the plot where his shop stood. They did not hear from him for a whole year, till one morning the postman cycled up to their doorstep with a letter from Bhajan Kaul. He had written a great deal about a jute business he had set up in Calcutta. 'Come and see for yourself,' the letter said. 'You can join the business if you like. If not, you can see the Howrah Bridge and the Victoria Memorial.'

Afreen had already seen the first and was not inclined to see the other.

She sat in the humid backseat of the taxi, clutching the plastic folder that had the letter from Bhajan, as well as the ones from her husband. She had read these innumerable times over the past week since she first got news of his disappearance and could now remember them word for word. For instance, in the second letter, he had described a trip to Dakshineshwar, the Kali temple south of the city where Bhajan had taken him:

> *I sat on one of the benches near the Ganga – I think they call it the Hooghly here – while Bhajan went inside the temple to do the puja. The day was very hot, the hottest since I've been here, but a cool breeze*

> *from the river kept me comfortable. It was so comfortable that I dozed off. (Guess what I was dreaming of?) I was woken up by a woman, an old woman. A Hindu widow, you could tell by the white sari. She was pleading with me to give her something – in the name of Kali! She had obviously not realized that I was Muslim. But how does that matter? If Hazratbal is holy, so is the Shankaracharya, isn't it? So, I gave her the money and you would not believe how good it felt. I was extravagant: I gave her Rs 10. I never felt better at having lost some money.*

He had to come to this awful city not because of the entreaties of Bhajan Kaul but because he was losing money. When the pandits moved out of Anantnag, the army moved in. Soon there were curfews for days and nights, and he could not even open his shop. Whenever the curfews were lifted so that people could go buy essentials, there were riots on the streets. It was difficult to predict when and how the troubles would start. You could be sitting at a tea stall in the market, having a conversation, when you would suddenly hear gunshots, and armoured vehicles and soldiers covered from head to toe in protective gear would be marching down the street in intimidating columns. What could you do if you were caught in such a place? Perhaps, you could run into one of the shops that were still open, before they pulled down their shutters. You could remain stuck in there for hours, while a pitched street battle progressed outside. From the lanes and by-lanes around the market, young men, their faces covered with cloth, would launch a counter-attack, raining pebbles and stone chips on the soldiers, while their cries of 'Azadi!' rent the air.

The troubles showed no signs of abating. It was impossible to calculate how much money they had lost. They had fallen back on the rent for their shop and their house. The situation was so bad that they were planning on moving to Delhi or Bombay, where they did not know anyone. So, when the letter from Bhajan Kaul arrived, the decision was made for them.

'As soon as I find my feet, I shall take you with me,' he had said. They were in bed, under the blankets.

He had remained silent for a few minutes before answering: 'We don't live in a paradise anymore.'

TWENTY-SEVEN

The furious ringing of the doorbell, rather than the cacophony of the neighbourhood municipal school, woke me the next morning. It was Ashutosh. He had not shaved or combed his hair and was wearing a shirt that had not been pressed. The ACP was in a foul mood.

'If you are done grieving for your boyfriend, can we get back to work?' he said, entering the flat without an invitation.

'What do you mean?' I managed to stammer.

He was standing with his arms on his hips, looking around disapprovingly at my unkempt drawing room. I was right behind him.

Without turning around, he said: 'I don't care whom you are fucking – woman, man, dog – as long as you remember that we have a job to do.'

'But you seem to have forgotten that,' he added, turning around to face me.

'No sir,' I uttered, hesitantly, 'it's just that…'

'Go and make tea,' my boss cut me off. 'A lot of it.'

When I returned a little later with a kettle and the only two unchipped china cups I possessed, I found him occupying the largest and the most comfortable sofa in the room, his feet on the rickety centre table. He had not even bothered to take off his shoes.

Ashutosh did not see me as he was reading a sheaf of papers. Another pile was on the table, on top of which was a large yellow envelope.

Seeing me, he pointed to it and said, 'That came for you.'

'What is this?'

'How should I know? Don't you see it is sealed?'

I put down the tray and picked up the envelope. My name and the address of the police headquarters at Lalbazaar were scrawled on it in a handwriting not unfamiliar to me.

'Tim Taylor?' Ashutosh asked. He was observing my expressions.

Without replying, I tore open the packet. About twenty-five to thirty photographs fell out. These were most definitely taken on the day of the Vasant Sena procession – the same day that Tim was murdered. I started going through them quickly, feeling confident that there would be something in these that would reveal to me who killed Tim.

The first few shots were of Vasant Sena members, singing and dancing down Theatre Road. There were also pictures of police officers, languid and disinterested, some of them listening to the radio. Though aesthetics were not really my primary concern now, I could not help noticing how cleverly Tim had framed his narrative, contrasting the hysterical energy of the devotees of Yogi Premananda with the lethargy of the state apparatus. It made me wonder if we had been underprepared that day, if we had underestimated the ability of the fanatical army to unleash violence of that magnitude.

After a dozen or so photographs came the prize shots: of the teenager firing the machine gun on Middleton Row. There was a fascinating sequence of a boy holding a gun above his head, screaming with all his body, aiming the muzzle at the camera. Now, I am no journalist, but even I could tell you that one or all of these would have made it to the front page of all the newspapers on the day after the rally. Maybe even tomorrow.

'So, this is what got him killed.'

Ashutosh was standing right behind me, looking at the photographs. His words echoed my thoughts.

'Where did this come from?' I asked.

The ACP picked up the envelope in which the photographs had come. It had the name Sapui & Sapui Studios printed on it. The address was 16B Ho Chi Minh Sarani.

'Let's go,' I said, looking around the room for my wallet and keys.

Ashutosh did not move an inch. 'Where do you want to go?' he said.

His question seemed very stupid to me, even irritated me.

'To this studio,' I replied, making no effort to conceal my irritation. 'Someone there was the last person to see Tim alive. They might have seen something.'

Ashutosh paid no heed to my nervous energy. Instead, he got up from the sofa and walked to the half-shut window of the room. He opened it, letting in all the noise of the street below.

He lit a cigarette and stood there, silently.

My impatience was rising like acid in my stomach. 'What are we waiting for?' I said after a minute or two.

The ACP spoke slowly, deliberately. 'If you go to the studio, maybe you will find out something or maybe you won't...'

'There is always that chance. But, does that mean we don't try at all?'

'No, that's not what I mean.'

'Then what?'

Ashutosh did not answer my question. He shut the window and put his finger on his lips to indicate that I should be quiet. Crossing the room, he put his hand on my shoulder and brought his mouth to my ear.

'What if I told you I know who killed Tim, and who has been killing the girls?'

'What do you mean?'

I did not realize that I had shouted. Ashutosh put his finger on his lips again. We heard the ringing of the municipal school bell in the neighbourhood and the voices of the children filled my dark, stuffy drawing room.

Clearing all the paper from the centre table, Ashutosh put an A4 sheet on it. The white paper had two lists of dates, inscribed in his nearly illegible handwriting. It looked something like this:

1.	November 15, 1988	November 7–10, 1988
2.	December 16, 1988	December 7–10, 1988
3.	January 9, 1989	January 5–10, 1989
4.	February 8, 1989	February 4–9, 1989
5.	March 10, 1989	March 5–9, 1989
6.		April 4–8, 1989
7.	May 6, 1989	May 4–8, 1989

8. June 2–5, 1989
9. July 1–6, 1989

'What am I looking at?' I asked him.

'You must be familiar with the first column,' said Ashutosh. 'You were the one who started compiling this.'

Perhaps my head was too muddled, but I could not figure it out.

'These are the dates on which the bodies of the girls were found,' said Ashutosh.

Now it became obvious. He had expanded my list to include an extra date – the one on which Aanchal Agarwal was found.

'What are the blank slots?' I said.

'You will see that one body was found every month since November last year. The empty slots are for the dates on which no body was found.'

'And, what are the dates on the right column?'

'We shall come to that in a bit, but first…'

The ACP looked around and found the light switch on the wall near the door. A yellow glow from the dirty bulb washed over the room, revealing the damp spots on the northwest corner of the ceiling and the plaster peeling beneath it. A lizard, surprised by the sudden disappearance of the darkness, scurried behind an old calendar that hung between two portraits of my parents.

'No reason for us to keep sitting in the dark,' he said, 'especially since we are so close to illumination.'

Ashutosh smiled, for the first time since he had arrived, perhaps thinking that his joke would get my usual enthusiastic response. In the police, when your boss makes a joke, you laugh, no matter how stupid you think it is. But I was getting impatient and this clandestine meeting in my room was too informal a setting for me to perform the usual role. Perhaps the ACP realized it, or perhaps he did not, but he replenished both our teacups from the kettle.

'Do you remember the day I sent you to meet Tim Taylor?' he said.

'Yes, of course.'

'Have you any idea what I was doing?'

'You told me: meeting the families of the dead girls.'

'Right, and you were supposed to meet me, do you remember?'

'The storm delayed me.'

Ashutosh smiled, knowingly, as if he was aware of something that I had not told him. 'Whatever your reasons were,' he continued. 'What do you think I was looking for?'

I took a moment before answering: 'You were looking for a pattern, something to connect the murders.'

'Excellent!' He lit another cigarette.

'Did you find anything?'

'Yes, I did. There was one thing that was common to the three families.'

'What was that?'

The ACP waited before answering. 'Vasant Sena,' he said. 'The three families were all members of it.'

This was perhaps a confirmation of everything I had suspected all along, but I did not know what to make of this information. What if the three families were members of Vasant Sena? What did that prove? Did it even mean anything, or was it simply a coincidence? Too many strings were still entangled to provide a clear narrative.

Ashutosh spoke slowly, as if trying to unentangle the strings. 'What was Tim doing in Calcutta?' he said.

'Reporting on the deaths of the girls?'

'No, no, that began in November. He was here since August last year.'

'Then?'

'I think,' said the ACP, 'he was keeping tabs on the Vasant Sena.'

The air in the room seemed to have suddenly become too heavy to breathe. My throat was choked. 'Do you think that's why he was killed?' I said.

'It is a possibility,' he replied. 'Some of the developments do point in that direction, though we don't yet have clear dots we can join. What we can say for sure is that the Vasant Sena did not want these pictures to go to the press. He also knew about their possible involvement in the black market organ trade.'

'What do you mean?'

'Remember Hope, the Vasant Sena devotee in Auckland that Tim had interviewed?'

Feeling even more claustrophobic, I went up to the window and opened it. The muddle in my head was clearing a little, but the skies outside were overcast. There was certainly going to be a downpour.

'But we cannot prove any of this in court,' I said.

'Not yet,' said Ashutosh, 'but there is more.'

He picked up the sheet of paper from the centre table and came to me. 'Look at the second list,' he said, giving it to me.

'What is this?'

'This is a list of the dates on which Dr Raktim Bose was apparently out of town, attending seminars.'

'Who's that?'

I thought I saw Ashutosh hesitating before answering my question. 'Rukmini's husband,' he said.

'What has he got to do with all of this?'

'It might seem a little far-fetched but it is not impossible,' he began. 'Dr Bose is a great devotee of Yogi Premananda. His whole family is. Besides his own practice, he heads the charity hospital of Vasant Sena. Also, he is a cardiac surgeon.'

This did seem a little far-fetched to me. 'What are you implying?' I said. 'Dr Bose killed the girls?'

'We know that the hearts of all the dead girls were removed surgically. It must have been done for a purpose.'

'What purpose?'

Ashutosh extinguished the cigarette he was smoking. 'Do you know the price of a human heart in the international market?'

This was a persuasive line of argument, but I was still not really convinced. Everything did not add up for me.

'All of this could be coincidental,' I said.

'Too many coincidences,' he said. 'Dr Bose, a cardiac surgeon and a Vasant Sena devotee, supposedly goes to seminars outside Calcutta every time a girl with her heart cut out turns up on our streets?'

'Yes, he was out of town and the girls were killed in town. A perfect alibi for him.'

'It would be the perfect alibi if he were actually where he said he would be. But, I checked on each seminar he was supposed to attend. What do you think I found?'

'That he was not at any of these seminars?'

'Even worse. None of the nine seminars he claims to have attended since November actually took place.'

The next suggestion I was about to make could have offended Ashutosh, but I went ahead anyway. 'Maybe he is having an affair,' I said, 'and trying to hide it from his wife.'

'Maybe he is,' said Ashutosh, 'or maybe he is not.'

'Where did you get his schedule?'

'Rukmini gave it to me.'

'You will still not be able to link it to Vasant Sena.'

'No, but we can at least try to stop Dr Bose.'

'You cannot prove that it is him even with what we have now.'

His face broke into a smile. 'You are right,' said Ashutosh, 'but I have more.'

Leaving me standing near the open window, he went back to the centre table, and started looking through the papers. The weather outside had turned worse, and it had begun raining. The ACP returned with another paper and handed it to me. It was a government report of some kind.

'What is this?' I asked.

'This is a report from the Department of Import and Export on how much Viaspan came into the country till March this year.'

'What is Viaspan?'

'Viaspan is the trademark under which the University of Wisconsin solution is sold. It is a preservation material used for organ transplant and storage. However, it is a very recent invention and is hardly used in India. The more popular alternative is Euro-Collins. But doctors are claiming that Viaspan could be the gold standard for organ preservation.'

'What are we getting at?'

Ashutosh lit another cigarette. 'Till March this year, India imported only twelve units of Viaspan,' he said. 'Now, take a wild guess as to who the importer could be?'

The tangled skein seemed a little more unknotted. 'Dr Bose?' I said.

'Well done,' he said. 'To be more precise, it is his hospital. That's what this report says. Now, why would the hospital need Viaspan? They don't do any organ transplants.'

There was enough to chew on now. We would still not be able to prove in a court that Dr Bose was the killer. There was after all nothing illegal about importing Viaspan. But, with what we had there was enough to get a search warrant for his hospital. If we found anything, we could arrest him, and once he was in a lock-up, hung upside down, a live wire in his penis, he would sing.

Ashutosh wanted to take all this to DCP Mukherjee. 'But I wanted to show it to you first,' he said. 'Now that you are convinced, let's go to the boss.'

We were almost out of the door when Ashutosh stopped me.

'Get your raincoat,' he said. 'It's pouring outside.'

TWENTY-EIGHT

If either of us had imagined that the DCP would be very happy with our discoveries or how Ashutosh had taken the investigation forward, we were proved wrong very soon. Not only did we fail to impress him, we also managed to piss him off completely. Having heard us out, and looked through our documents, he lit his pipe, slowly, deliberately, and fixed his deprecating gaze upon us. What Ashutosh thought I cannot tell, but I felt myself crumbling beneath it.

The DCP waited for a few minutes before the firing began. 'There is already an official investigation going on in this case,' he said. 'So what reason did you have to conduct a private one?'

Ashutosh tried to explain something but he was cut off immediately. 'You think you have become Detective Byomkesh Bakshi? Where do you think you are? In a crime fiction novel?' the DCP continued. 'Maybe we should just let you go from the department, and you can be a private investigator then.'

'Sir, please allow me to explain myself,' the ACP said.

'I don't want to hear anything Ashutosh,' the DCP shouted. 'This is gross insubordination.' The volume in which the last sentence was spat out revealed how angry he was, and it could put even someone as dauntless as Ashutosh on the back foot.

'Sir?'

'You were supposed to apprise me of every little development in the investigation. What do you mean by concealing all this from me for so long?'

Ashutosh's strategy in responding to the machine gun of the DCP's questions and accusations was to speak in a low, calm voice. 'My intentions were never to conceal anything from you, sir,' he said, 'but I did not want to come to you without something substantial.'

This seemed to piss off the DCP even more. 'Substantial?' he thundered. 'You call this substantial? This is absolute rubbish.'

'Sir?'

'You have put together a cock and bull story, based on absolutely circumstantial evidence that will be thrown out of any court in two minutes. Why do you want to embarrass the department like this?'

'I know this isn't enough, but...'

'You think any judge will issue an arrest warrant with this nonsense?'

'Not an arrest warrant, sir, but definitely a search warrant.'

'A search warrant? For what?'

'For the Vasant Sena hospital at Jadavpur run by Dr Bose.'

When the DCP heard this, the floodgates of his anger seemed to break. He kept screaming at us for nearly a minute, his face turning purple. I feared he would have a stroke. When he finally stopped, exhausted and out of breath, it seemed as if someone had used a vacuum pump to suck all sounds out of the room. All that one could hear was the buzzing of the air-conditioner.

'You are off this case immediately,' the DCP said, pointing an accusatory finger at Ashutosh. 'So are you,' he added, turning to me.

'No, sir,' replied Ashutosh, without missing a breath. 'You cannot take us off this case.'

The ACP's voice had changed completely. It had turned defiant, immediately depriving the DCP's orders of any authority. The latter's face betrayed the shock he experienced at this attitude of a subordinate.

'What the fuck do you mean?' he screamed. 'You are off the case. No discussions.'

Ashutosh spoke slowly, ensuring that the DCP understood every word he was saying. 'If you take either of us off this case, we will call a press conference and present all this evidence to the journalists. They can do what they want with it.'

Given his wheatish complexion, one might have imagined that the DCP's face could not turn more purple, but it did, taking on an ugly shade, like a burnt eggplant about to burst. He was unable to say anything for a few minutes, and his breathing seemed to be troubled. Improper as it might have been, I found the situation exceedingly humorous.

We had won the first round.

But, we should not have forgotten that the DCP was our boss, and he had enough resources at his disposal to turn the tables quite easily. That is exactly what he did in a minute.

All the anger, the purpleness, leaked away from his face, and his lips transformed themselves into the shape of a smile. The metamorphosis was quite disturbing, at least for me.

'Why don't both of you sit down?' he said, almost pleasantly.

We had been standing since we entered the room fifteen minutes ago. The DCP had always been in the mood to dismiss us summarily. Since that did not happen, he was now addressing us in a mollifying tone, almost paternal.

Ashutosh tried to say something, but the DCP indicated with his outstretched palm that he should not.

'You can call a press conference if you like,' he said. 'There is nothing I can do to stop you. But there is nothing you can do either to stop me from calling another press conference.'

He was smiling like a cat, a very satisfied one. The DCP's expression told us that what he had said should have been enough for us, if we were smart. It was not enough, at least for me.

'It is hard when your wife is fucking someone else,' said the DCP, looking straight at Ashutosh. Though he was still smiling, his voice was steely. 'It is hard, I know,' he continued, 'but this department is not at your disposal to settle scores with your rivals in love.'

The DCP's face hardened over the last sentence. 'Is it love that's driving you crazy Ashutosh? Did you think I would not know that you are fucking Dr Bose's wife?'

He paused, possibly for dramatic effect. Ashutosh was sitting on my right. I had an intense desire to turn around and look at him, but I did not dare.

'Now, this is what we are going to do,' the DCP said. 'You are going to leave all this – all this evidence – with me. You are going to apply for leave. Not too long, for a week or so. Go to Darjeeling if you like. When you return from your holiday, I'll assign you to a new case. You have become too personally involved in this one to have any professional detachment. I cannot allow you to continue with this. Are we clear?'

Ashutosh did not reply. Instead, he stood up, saluted the DCP and walked out of the room. I was about to follow him when the DCP indicated with his fingers that he wanted me to keep sitting.

For a minute or more, he kept staring at me as he lit his pipe and smoked. This period of being observed made me intensely uncomfortable.

'Are you familiar with Section 377 of the Indian Penal Code?' he said at length.

'Yes, sir,' I muttered, my heart racing like crazy.

'Then you must also be aware that you are in contravention of it.'

I did not reply, but averted my eyes, looking down at my shoes.

'You faggot!' The DCP got up from his chair with such violence that it fell backwards. For a moment I thought he would climb over the table and attack me like a wild animal, but he did not do anything of the sort. Instead he just stood there, looking down at me like one looks at a rat.

'Have you forgotten who you work for?' he screamed. 'Have you forgotten why I assigned you to Ashutosh?'

'No, sir.' I still did not look up.

'Then why do I have no report of what he has been up to?'

'I did not know sir.'

'It is your fucking job to know. Are you telling me that you cannot do your job?'

'No, sir.'

'Do you know what will happen to you if I withdraw my protection? Do you know what they do to faggots like you in Alipore Jail? Is that where you want to end up?'

'No, sir.'

My whole body was shaking. Though I tried my best to not show it, the DCP's eyes did not miss it. It seemed he had exhausted his anger and sat down. He continued talking to me in an even voice: 'If you want me to continue protecting you, you must do your work. I want a report at the end of every day on what Ashutosh is doing, where he is going, whom he is meeting, and what they are talking about. Be his shadow and keep me informed. I don't want another surprise like this. Do you understand?'

My voice had lost all its power, so I nodded in affirmation. The DCP dismissed me. In the open veranda outside his office, I found that my hands and legs were still shaking, and my breath was slow and uneven. The weather had also changed for the worse. Though it was only afternoon, the skies were completely dark, and it was raining.

Ashutosh was waiting outside for me and he wanted to know why I had been held up. I confessed everything to him, including the fact that my primary duty involved surveillance on him. The ACP seemed to find this very amusing. 'Let's go then,' he said.

'Where?'

'To Dr Bose's hospital. There is a patient I want to interview.'

'But we were just told not to investigate this case.'

Ashutosh smiled and lit a cigarette. 'You can either come with me and find out whom I am meeting and what we are talking about, just like the boss told you,' he said, 'or not.'

'If I go with you, I'll have to report it.'

'You are a smart man, Pradip. I'm sure you will find a way to do it without jeopardising our investigation.'

There was no denying that this offer made me very excited, but I had a lingering doubt. 'Do you trust me?' I said.

Ashutosh did not answer my question, and I would never have the opportunity to find out what he thought. He patted my shoulder and blew rings of smoke.

TWENTY-NINE

The landlord showed Afreen into the one-bedroom flat where her husband had apparently lived for the past six to seven months. As she entered the musty apartment, something struck her as odd immediately: it did not look at all like a place inhabited by the person she knew so intimately. There was nothing to suggest that he had lived here so long. None of his clothes or belongings remained in the empty cupboards. In fact, it seemed to her that someone had done a thorough cleaning job after him, removing every little object or item that could have betrayed his existence. It was as if her husband had never lived in this flat. It had been inhabited by a stranger.

'Did anyone clean up this place?' she asked the landlord. The question was redundant: there were cobwebs hanging from the corners of the ceiling, and a thin layer of dust covered the furniture. Yet, she asked this question thinking that someone might have tampered with her husband's possessions – stolen some things – and rendered the place unrecognisable.

'No,' replied the landlord, 'I thought we should wait for you.'

The landlord was standing near the entrance of the flat, nervously fiddling with the keys in his left hand. He was a middle-aged Bengali man who had introduced himself as Sabyasachi Khan. His appearance was mostly unremarkable, except for the chest-length beard of the haji. It had recently been given a new coat of henna. He wore a checked half-sleeved shirt and navy blue trousers that had obviously not been tailored well enough for his bulky form. Afreen observed that dark patches of sweat were forming under his armpits.

As she stood under a creaking fan in the centre of the room, Khan started narrating to her how his tenant had disappeared suddenly.

'He was quite reticent, a private person, as you must know,' he said. 'He would go out very early in the morning and return only late at night. Even when he was home on Sundays, we did not really hear him.'

The only way Khan and his wife, who lived in the flat on the floor above, knew that their tenant was home was on the infrequent occasion when he turned on the radio. He usually listened to bhajans.

'Bhajans?' Afreen was surprised to hear this. She had never known her husband to listen to any sort of devotional music, leave alone bhajans.

'We were quite surprised as well,' the landlord said. 'This is not the kind of music we hear very often in this part of town. The neighbours were wondering if we had rented the flat out to a Hindu.'

On most days, however, there was no music from the flat. One could see a big lock hanging outside the door. Khan possessed a key to this lock, but since his tenant was always so regular with the rent and other expenses, he had never had any reason to make enquiries.

'Perhaps, I should have taken more interest in what he was doing and where he was going,' Khan told Afreen. 'Who can tell when he went missing?'

'How did you find out?'

'It was a Wednesday,' Khan said, 'two days after the army had been called in to quell a riot in the city.'

For three or four days, there was curfew on the streets, but on that morning, a police van had gone around the area announcing that the restrictions had been temporarily lifted and people could step out of their homes for a few hours if they wanted to. As rations in his house were running low, Khan decided to take advantage of this opportunity to go out and buy some eggs, bread and milk. While climbing down the stairs, he found the door to this flat locked. This struck him as strange: where could his tenant have gone? Khan presumed he must have also stepped out to buy rations, but when he returned a couple of hours later, he found the door still locked. This made him uneasy. All through that day and the next, he checked repeatedly, climbing down the stairs every time only to find the lock still hanging on the door. It was obvious that the tenant had not returned home.

On the third day, finding the door still locked, he called some of the neighbours and consulted them on what he should do. Most of them advised him to inform the police, but a few said that the tenant might have simply gone home and there was no need to panic. One of them suggested that since Khan had the key to the flat anyway, he might as well go in and see if everything was alright. The harried landlord felt that this was the most prudent course of action.

When Khan found that the clothes and other objects in the flat were missing, he felt relatively certain that his tenant had gone home.

'The rent for this month is pending, but I am not worried about that,' he said. 'Your husband had given me a deposit that is more than enough to cover the rent and other expenses. Thankfully, he had given me your number, so I was able to call you up. It is good that you are here now. You can take all the decisions.'

Khan sat down on a chair near the door and started wiping the sweat on his face with a checked handkerchief.

Afreen did not know what decision she was expected to make. A call from a stranger, now sitting in front of her, had informed her that her husband had gone missing in Calcutta. She had lived all her life in Srinagar, never going any further south than Shimla. Her friends and family, even her in-laws, advised her not to go looking for him. They told her she knew nothing of big cities, that it was futile to search for people who did not want to be found, and that if he wanted to be with her, he would surely turn up sometime or the other. She had ignored their collective wisdom, but now as she stood here, in the centre of this room, utterly clueless about what she would do, she wondered if they had been right.

'Did you inform the police?' she asked Khan.

'No. What would I tell the police? I did not even have his photograph.'

On hearing this, Afreen took out a black-and-white photograph of her husband that she carried around in her purse. It was taken before their wedding. She remembered looking at it, before she had ever seen him, and wondering what this stranger with whom she had agreed to spend all her life would be like. Now, as she looked at the photograph, she felt like she was looking at a stranger again.

'I think we should go to the police,' she said.

At the Park Circus police station, there was utter chaos. The constable responsible for taking down FIRs was an emaciated and overworked man, afflicted by chronic ill-temper. He sat in an uncomfortable chair, behind a large and dusty wooden table with unsteady legs. A precarious tower of folders grew on the table, with crumpled yellow pages sticking out. A clamouring crowd of plaintiffs milled around, asking for their complaints to be noted in the police register. Finally, after the mediation of a senior officer, they agreed to stand in a serpentine queue, starting at the table and winding its way out of the police station. They approached the constable one by one to get their complaints registered.

Khan and Afreen stood in the queue for a couple of hours before their turn came. She was thankful that he had come with her, as she did not feel confident that she could deal with everything herself. When their turn finally came, it was Khan who spoke to the constable.

The conversation took place in Bengali. Afreen did not understand a word, but Khan narrated it to me later.

'We are here to lodge a missing person complaint,' Khan said.

'Who's missing?' asked the constable without even looking up.

'My tenant.'

'So, what is it? He has run away without paying rent?'

'No, that's not the problem.'

'Why don't you find a new tenant?'

At this point the constable looked up and the expression on his face changed, as it often does when a Hindu sees a Muslim.

'This is his wife,' Khan said, introducing Afreen.

'A relative of yours?' the constable asked.

'No sir, I am a Bengali.'

Khan had thought this was explanation enough, but the constable did not seem to understand. He kept looking at them with questioning eyes. 'They are from Kashmir,' Khan explained.

'Kashmir,' the constable repeated. 'Since when has he been missing?'

Khan told him the dates. The constable's face suddenly became animated. 'Aren't those…' he checked his calendar, where a few dates were circled in red. Then, in a self-congratulatory tone, he said: 'Exactly! That's the date right after the riot. Are you sure he was not involved in some trouble?'

'Not at all, sir,' Khan replied. 'He was a very nice, quiet man.'

The constable put down his pen and looked at Khan. 'How long did you know him?'

'A couple of months, sir.'

'Do you even know what is happening in Kashmir? Very nice and quiet young men are going and joining terrorists. Some even come to Calcutta, before escaping to Bangladesh, and then travelling to Pakistan for training. How do you know your tenant was not one of them?'

The constable's voice had grown louder. Though Khan thought he was talking utter rubbish, he replied as deferentially as possible. 'Forgive me sir, but if we knew terrorists, why would we come to you?' he said.

This seemed to make some sense to the constable. He looked from Khan to Afreen and back, and said in Hindi, possibly for her benefit, 'Do you have a photograph?'

Afreen took out a photograph from her purse and gave it to the constable. He looked at it and put it in his folder.

'What is his name?' he asked.

She replied: 'Muzammil Ibrahim.'

THIRTY

The Yogi Brahmananda Charitable Hospital is at Jadavpur. You must be aware that though Jadavpur is now obviously a part of south Calcutta, we have no jurisdiction over it. Everything beyond Selimpur is under the jurisdiction of the West Bengal Police.

(Is that why they wanted to set up the hospital there? Perhaps you are right, but the official reason they gave was that land was cheaper in the area.)

On our way to the hospital Ashutosh explained to me why we were going there, though we did not have a warrant and could not possibly conduct an official enquiry. He wanted to meet Asima Chatterjee, the mother of Anasuya Chatterjee, one of the murdered girls. He had seen her briefly at her husband Asim Chatterjee's flat, when he had gone to interview them. Asim had not allowed Ashutosh to meet her, stating that she was unwell. Now, Asima was a patient in the psychiatric ward of the hospital.

'How did you find out that she is there?' I wanted to know.

Ashutosh was driving his blue Ambassador; I was sitting beside him. He answered without looking at me: 'When I first saw her, I thought there was something she wanted to tell me, but her husband did not let her. So, I kept looking out for an opportunity when I could meet her alone.'

The opportunity presented itself when Asim travelled to East Berlin the previous month. He usually went there on business once every two or three months,.

'But when I went to their flat,' said the ACP, 'the security guards told me she was not there.'

Our car stopped at a traffic snarl on Dhakuria Bridge. Though I was not thinking of it then, we must have been near the spot where, a few years ago, Vasant Sena members had been attacked and killed by unidentified assailants.

Ashutosh continued with his narrative:

'A few days after my visit, Asima had an episode. She climbed to the roof of the building in which they lived and, standing on the parapet, threatened to jump off if her daughter was not brought to her immediately. No one was able to convince her to get off. The police and the fire department had to be called. It took considerable coaxing and cajoling from her friends and relatives, especially her husband, before she agreed to climb down.'

The cars had started moving again, but progress was slow. We stopped twice before we got off the bridge on South Gariahat Road.

The guards at the building, who were Ashutosh's source, told him that Asima had disappeared after this incident. It was as if she had become a ghost. Her husband, too, rarely ventured out of the flat, and everyone assumed that he was taking care of his indisposed wife. A fortnight or so passed. Then one morning, a black van arrived near the gates of the building. It was driven by a man in a white uniform, and he was accompanied by a team of paramedics. Asim was waiting for them at the gate. They went up to his flat. The guard had felt there was something odd about their surreptitious movements, but he could not put his finger on it. They came down about half an hour later. Asima was also with them. She was not walking; they had put her in a wheelchair. The guard went forward to offer help, but Asim shooed him away. The small party, including Asim, got into the van and drove away.

'But how did you find out which hospital they took her to?' I said.

Ashutosh explained that the van that took Asima away had the name of the hospital painted on its side. The guard had seen it and remembered.

On reaching the hospital, Ashutosh parked his car on the opposite side of the road. There was a large crowd at the gate, comprising mostly people from the slums around the city and the suburbs. Such crowds are not uncommon in front of government facilities that provide free services. Ashutosh told me that this one also did, but only for Vasant Sena members.

The gates were guarded by a private security contingent that was checking every person before allowing them to enter.

'We will never get past the security,' I said. 'They will know in a minute that we are not Vasant Sena members.'

'Do you think I did not plan this?' he replied in an irritated voice.

He had already taken an appointment with the psychiatry department and thought of proper identities for both of us. I was supposed to be the patient, suffering from acute depression since the death of my wife a few months back. (It was not a role that would be difficult for me to perform; Ashutosh had perhaps thought of all this.) The ACP would be my elder brother.

Since we were not seeking free services, we did not have to jostle through the crowd. We had access to a side entrance that was free of all the chaos and dirt usually associated with service provided gratis.

Even at this gate, there was considerable security and our appointment slip was checked before we could enter. A Vasant Sena guard frisked us thoroughly.

The hospital grounds were surprisingly empty. We crossed a patch of grass, lush and neatly mowed, before entering a large rectangular building. It was air-conditioned and smelled of formaldehyde and lavender. Ashutosh pointed to a brass plaque on a wall near the entrance. The inscription on it thanked businessman Hari Agarwal for a generous donation to this institute.

'Do you know who that is?' Ashutosh whispered to me.

Of course I knew Hari Agarwal. The business tycoon was the father of Aanchal Agarwal, one of the murdered girls.

The inside of this building was almost like a maze, with an endless number of corridors and staircases. The air conditioning kept the temperature low, in stark contrast to the muggy weather outside, so low in fact that my palms started turning cold and I had to stick them in my pockets. Another odd feature was there were hardly any windows. One would have to walk along stark walls, painted a very light shade of blue. In the absence of natural light, the only source of illumination was the faint white tube lights hanging from steel brackets in the ceilings, at equal distances from each other. These barely managed to illuminate the corridors. Even when you reached the rare window, you would find it barred with iron grilles, possibly intended to keep people from escaping or entering. It seemed to me that the architectural design of the place was intended for a soporific, claustrophobic effect.

To reach the psychiatric department, we had to go through paediatrics. It was quite crowded with parents and their wards waiting in the corridors. The scene here was unlike in any other paediatrics department I had ever seen. Only a few children were sitting with their parents; most were running around and creating a ruckus, and the corridor was filled with such noise and shouting that it would deafen anyone. The other thing I noticed was that all the patients were girls. The oldest among them would have been about fourteen, the youngest barely eight or nine. There had formed different groups and were playing different games as they awaited their turn to be called in for an examination. Some were playing hide-and-seek, a few were chasing each other. One group had formed a train and were going round and round, whistling and shouting. The doctors and nurses did not seem to mind the uproar at all. In fact, a couple of ward boys had joined the game, acting as railway guards, stopping the train at imaginary stations, and inviting other girls to join in. They even had red and green flags. It was an amazing sight.

'What's going on?' Ashutosh asked a man who was standing in a corner.

He turned around and looked at us with a bemused expression as if only an imbecile would ask such a question. 'Is this your first time?' he said.

'Yes.'

'Well, I was surprised too when I saw it the first time. Now, I am used to it. This is a good way to keep the children busy as they await their turns.'

'Turn for what?'

'For their check-up, what else? Isn't that why we are here, to get our daughters checked?'

'What is wrong with your daughter?'

'Nothing, thank the Yogi.'

'Then why are you here for a check-up?'

The man's expression turned even more inscrutable. 'This is the regular monthly check-up. It is mandatory for daughters of all Vasant Sena members. The Yogi says that in our country girls are not given proper nutrition and they grow up to be weak women. So, he has made it compulsory for all of us to bring our daughters in for a monthly check-up.'

The man looked around for something. 'Where is your daughter?' he said.

'I don't have a daughter,' said Ashutosh to him, repeating our ruse.

The man looked at me with genuine sympathy in his eyes. 'The Yogi will make everything alright,' he said.

The girl who was the engine of the train let out a shrill whistle.

It took us about ten more minutes to find the psychiatry department. At its entrance, we were met by a nurse who wanted to know the purpose of our visit.

'We are here to see Mrs Asima Chatterjee,' said Ashutosh.

'Why?'

'I'm Dr Singh and this is Dr Batabyal. We are here to conduct an advanced diagnosis.'

The nurse looked through her register. 'There is nothing in here about your visit,' she said.

'That's very irregular,' said Ashutosh, introducing a subtle strain of irritation in his voice.

'I cannot let you meet her without an appointment.'

Ashutosh made a cluckling sound, to express annoyance. He looked at her directly in the eyes and said, 'Sister, you realize this is utter bureaucratic inefficiency. How can you prevent a doctor from meeting his patient because some idiot forgot to write it down?'

'I'm sorry sir,' the nurse stammered, 'but I need to verify it.'

She immediately picked up the phone and dialled a number. I don't know about Ashutosh, but as I stood there, I felt some difficulty in breathing, possibly out of nervousness. What consequences would we face if we were caught? What would DCP Mukherjee do with us? But as they say, fortune favours the brave, and now, she favoured us a little. No one picked up the phone at the other end.

'Who are you trying to get through to?' Ashutosh said.

'Dr Ankit Banerjee, the head of the department.'

'Dr Banerjee was my batchmate at the medical college,' said Ashutosh without missing a beat. His ability to come up with these stories amazed me.

The nurse dialled the number again, with the same result. Ashutosh looked at his watch impatiently, and then spoke to the nurse, 'We are getting late, sister. Will you kindly go and call him yourself while we wait here?'

The nurse looked at Ashutosh with uncertainty in her eyes, but then her resolve seemed to weaken, and she abandoned her post and hurried away. No sooner had she gone than Ashutosh began to scan her register. 'Room no. 71,' he declared, looking up.

Asima Chatterjee was the sole occupant of the room, though it could have easily accommodated two patients. There were, in fact, two single, iron beds in the room. She was wearing a loose, green, hospital gown and sitting in a comfortable chair, staring out at the torrential rain. The window in her room also had iron grilles.

'Mrs Chatterjee,' said Ashutosh.

She turned around to look at us. There was no expression on her face or in her eyes, she might as well have been drugged.

'How are you feeling today?' he continued.

She did not answer. I was starting to fear that she was gone too far and would not be able to tell us anything. Ashutosh asked her a few more questions, generic ones about her health, but she did not say anything, only stared at us with vacuous eyes.

Then something remarkable happened. Though we were at some distance from the paediatrics department, we heard the loud whistle of the children's train and the sound of laughter. This seemed to attract Asima's attention and animate her.

'What is that?' she said.

'Children playing,' replied Ashutosh.

'Will you take me there? My daughter must also be with them.'

'Your daughter?'

'Yes, my daughter Anasuya. She must be playing with the other children. She loves being the engine of their train.'

Ashutosh went down on his knees so that he was on the same eye level as Asima. 'Don't you remember what happened to your daughter?' he said.

'Yes,' she replied. 'We took her to the ashram. Asim said she would stay with the Yogi for a few days.'

'Yogi Premananda?'

She nodded her head to indicate that it was indeed him. The sound of the children's laughter and the whistle of the train drifted to us again. It seemed closer now.

'Why did you take her to the ashram?' said Ashutosh.

'The Yogi needed her.'

'For what?'

'For the ritual.'

'What ritual?'

Asima got up from her chair and walked up to the window. 'On those nights every month when there is no moon, the Yogi performs the ritual that will make him immortal.'

She paused for a moment. 'For this, he needs young girls,' she said.

'Why does he need girls?'

Asima did not say anything for a minute. Turning around, she fixed her gaze on us. But the gaze was no longer glassy. In an almost inaudible whisper, she said: 'He eats their hearts.'

The room seemed to have become colder suddenly, as if someone had turned down the air conditioning. The lights had also become dimmer. The whistle of the children's train was alarmingly close, as if it would run us over.

THIRTY-ONE

The body of the twelfth girl washed up near Princep Ghat on September 30, 1989. How am I so sure of the number? Call it a policeman's intuition, if you will. Yes, there were some bodies we would never be able to trace, and at least one that would remain unidentified. But, by the logic of the murders, this had to be the penultimate one. This is, of course, in retrospective analysis. Then, we did not know how many girls had been murdered and how many more were to come. Asima had given us some vital information, but we were yet to devise a mechanism that would allow us to predict the next murder.

When the news of the discovery of the body reached us, we were at Embassy Bar on Lenin Sarani. What? What? Yes, yes, this was the same bar where the singer called Sunita was killed. What? Why would I deny it? It was me who told you about it. Ashutosh had shot her in the middle of a brawl. The place had remained shut for a few days while the police investigated the case, but seriously, who cares for a dead pub singer? A couple of weeks after the incident, the shady establishment reopened, and though they did away with the musical entertainment, regulars such as Ashutosh returned.

After interviewing Asima, we had gone straight to Embassy, and had continued talking and drinking through the night, trying to figure out the meaning of what we had learned from her. I told him of what I had seen at the burning ghat. This must be a ritual neither of us knew about. At the ghat, the holy man seemed to revive a dead girl by eating the heart of a goat. Why could Premananda not perform a similar ritual, where he ate the heart of young girls? After all, many religions demand sacrifice – sometimes even self-sacrifice, from the most ardent followers.

Ashutosh remained sceptical. He argued that one could not transfer life from one creature to another or make oneself immortal by eating someone's heart. Perhaps what Asima had told us was the hallucination of an unwell mind? And even if we were to believe that the Yogi was conducting such a ritual every new moon, there had to be a different motive behind it: 'A commercial motive,' insisted Ashutosh.

'There are only two reasons for murder – love and money,' he said, repeating his old theory. 'Since passion that can lead to murder is rare, the only plausible motive is money.'

Ashutosh said we needed to figure out the mercenary motive to untangle this case. In my inebriated state, induced by night-long consumption of cheap whisky, I was only half-listening to him when the telephone at the bar rang. Ram Bahadur, the night guard, who was dozing on a bar stool, received the call. It was for Ashutosh. Someone was calling from the Lalbazaar control room.

How did the caller know where we were? Well, you see, every senior officer in the police force has a network of informers within the department, who act as his eyes and ears. You could not possibly get anything done without such a network. The constable who called that morning knew exactly where to find Ashutosh, and how important the information he had was for the ACP.

I could not hear the conversation from where I was sitting, but I could see that it made Ashutosh agitated. The ACP slammed the receiver on the cradle and hurried back to the table. 'Let's go,' he barked at me.

'What happened?'

'Another dead girl has been found.'

He picked up his half-filled glass and drained it. I followed suit, but when I was putting the empty glass back on the wooden table, I found that my hand was shaking.

As we would later find out, the body was discovered by fifty-five-year-old cloth merchant Laxminarayan Poddar. Every Monday, Poddar went to the Princep Ghat to take a dip in the Ganga and perform a puja for his mother, who had died the previous year. He usually arrived at the ghat before dawn to avoid crowds, and was always accompanied by his driver, Bhola Singh. When Laxminarayan went down to the river, Bhola would park the Mercedes by the side of the road and wait patiently behind the wheel. He would usually not have to wait longer than ten to fifteen minutes, but his instructions were to keep the air conditioner in the car running full blast. His employer could not tolerate the heat and the dust, and would hurriedly seek refuge in the cool interiors of the car, once his religious duties had been performed.

This morning, they got late because of the downpour that had not stopped since the previous night. They waited for the intensity of the rain to abate before setting out. When they finally reached the ghat, wrestlers were already exercising in the mud pits and a couple of juice sellers were setting up their stalls. Laxminarayan muttered impatiently while getting out of the car, and Bhola thought he would take longer than usual, so imagine his surprise when he spotted his employer in the rear-view mirror after a couple of minutes, running towards the car, bare bodied, his dhoti trailing behind him.

Bhola jumped out of his seat and ran towards Laxminarayan who was obviously shocked and muttering incomprehensively. The driver held his hand and asked what had happened but the cloth merchant could only cry: 'Dead!'

Accompanied by a few wrestlers and the juice sellers, Bhola Singh went to the ghat to find out what had frightened his employer. It didn't take him too long. At the spot where the marble steps of the ghat met the dark waters of the river, a human body was bobbing up and down on the waves. Though the body was bloated, Bhola could see instantly that it belonged to a girl, barely ten or twelve years old. A deadweight tied with a string to the girl's right toe had caught the anchor of a country boat moored nearby. The boatmen would have spotted her at daybreak if they had spent the night in their vessels as usual, but because of the rain and storm they had slept in rooms along the ghat the previous night.

Bhola took charge of the situation; he was accustomed to being in the driver's seat. He sent two wrestlers running to the

Babughat police station and asked one of the boatmen to take a vessel out and find the river police patrol. As the body had been found in the water, it would probably be their jurisdiction. After dispatching everyone on these errands, Bhola went down the slippery steps of the ghat carefully and caught hold of the string tied to the toe of the dead girl. It was the sharp strong kind used to fly kites. He tied the string around his finger and sat on the steps, on his haunches, to prevent the body from floating away with the current. That's the position in which the police found him, on the edge of the dark, muddy river.

It took us less than half an hour from Lenin Sarani to the Babughat police station. After a night of rain, the morning was bleak, and the streets were empty. The sanitation workers had played truant, so all the vats and dumping points were overflowing with garbage. Little rivulets of dirty water, carrying soggy paper, polythene and shit, flowed from these to join the bigger streams in drains, all of which would eventually merge with the river. The air was heavy with their stink; the roads were muddy and slippery and difficult to drive on. As we were crossing Mayo Road, we came upon a municipal truck, one of those used to sprinkle water on the streets in the morning. It had turned over on its side. A contingent of traffic police was already there, so we did not stop.

As soon as Ashutosh saw the face of the girl, he let out a howl, like an animal in pain, and started cursing loudly. We were in a small, sunless room at the Babughat police station, where the body of the girl was kept. A forty-watt naked bulb was hanging from the ceiling by a wire. That was the only source of illumination in the room, but it failed miserably in its purpose, and darkness colonized its far corners. The room had a dank, stuffy smell.

'What happened?' I was completely taken aback by Ashutosh, especially in my half-drunk, sleep-deprived, groggy state.

The ACP held me by the hand and dragged me to the body. 'Look at her carefully,' he said. 'Can you recognize her?'

I knew the girl immediately. We had seen her yesterday at the hospital. She was the engine of the children's train.

The blood in my veins rushed to my head. I cried out in horror.

'We could have saved her,' said Ashutosh.

His voice was lower, but harder. It was as if suddenly, his anger had become a cold, hard metal.

'Has the body been identified?' he asked the on-duty sub-inspector, who was standing near the door.

'Yes,' he replied. 'Her name is Sukanya Choudhuri, age twelve years. She went missing a few days back. Her parents filed a missing report.'

'Do you have copy of the report? Can I see it?'

'Yes, sir, we have it in the office.'

We followed the sub-inspector to the office, where he let us see the report. It said that Sukanya was a student of Calcutta Girls' School. The date on the report was September 25 – but we had seen her alive, playing with the other children only the day before, September 29.

'Are her parents here?' Ashutosh said.

The parents were waiting in an adjoining room, impassive, like stone statues. Ashutosh introduced himself and pulled up a chair.

'I'm terribly sorry for your loss,' he said, 'but you realize we need to start investigations immediately. I have a few questions, if you don't mind.'

The father nodded his head. Ashutosh took out a notepad and a pencil from his pocket.

'Name?'

'Suniti Kumar Choudhuri.' His voice was surprisingly steady.

'Profession?'

'I teach chemistry at Jadavpur University.'

'A man of science! Surely you don't believe in superstitions?'

'What do you mean?'

'We shall find out soon enough.'

Ashutosh turned to Professor Choudhuri's wife. 'What is your name, madam?' he asked.

She seemed startled by the question and turned towards her husband. He put his hand on hers.

'Jayati Choudhuri,' she said.

'Do you work?'

'No, I am a housewife.'

'Very well,' said Ashutosh, getting up from the chair. Though his voice and movements were steady, I could tell that he was deeply agitated.

'How many children do you have?' he asked.

'We have a son and a daughter,' Suniti replied.

Ashutosh stared at him for a moment. 'Well, your daughter is dead now,' he said. 'So you only have a son, isn't it?'

I thought this was a rather insensitive line of questioning, but I knew better than to interrupt Ashutosh.

'Yes,' said the bereaved father in an almost inaudible tone.

The ACP sat down again. 'I've two more questions. First, you are a member of Vasant Sena, isn't it?'

Both Suniti and Jayati stared at him with blank eyes. 'What has that got to do with anything?' the husband said.

'Doesn't it?'

'I don't understand.'

Ashutosh laughed, ironically. 'You will very soon, I assure you. Just answer my question. Are you and your wife members of Vasant Sena or not?'

Suniti took a deep breath. 'Yes, we are, so what?' he said.

'I thought so,' said the ACP. 'Now here is my second question. I am a little confused: You filed the missing report on September 25, right?'

'Yes, when she did not return from school…'

'Exactly, exactly, and yet, she was alive yesterday.'

An almost imperceptible cloud passed over Professor Choudhuri's face. 'What do you mean?' he said.

'My colleague here,' said Ashutosh pointing to me, 'and I saw her yesterday. She was healthy, and happy, and playing with other children. Do you know where?'

'I've no idea what you are talking about.'

'You don't, do you?'

Before the man could answer the question, Ashutosh had grabbed his collar, lifted him from the chair, and flung him across the room. Professor Choudhuri, nearly six feet tall but much leaner than the ACP, seemed to fly across the distance and crash into a couple of chairs kept a few feet away.

Ashutosh pounced on the hapless man and started raining punches on him. It took both the sub-inspector and me to pull him back. His victim lay on the floor for a minute before pulling himself up, holding on to the broken chairs. His nose was bleeding and his upper lip was cut. Staggering a little, Suniti spat out a mouthful of blood on the dirty floor, and sat down on a bench, far away from Ashutosh.

'Why did you do it?' the ACP shouted at him.

The man did not answer. He was coughing, trying to get back his breath.

'Why did you do it?' Ashutosh screamed again.

'What did he do, sir?' the sub-inspector said. He was trying desperately to take charge of the situation, but with the sudden turn of events, found himself completely at sea.

'He has killed his daughter and cut out her heart.'

The sub-inspector stared at Ashutosh as if he was looking at a mad man. The ACP did indeed look completely possessed and out of control. I had spent many months with him but had never seen him in such a state.

Free from our restraining grip, the ACP charged at Suniti again, but this time, the wife threw herself between them.

'What are you trying to do?' she cried. 'Are you trying to kill him?'

'Yes,' replied Ashutosh, without a shade of mercy in his voice. 'And, I will kill you too, if you don't tell me right now why you killed your daughter.'

'We killed her for the Yogi.'

It was not Jayati who gave the answer, but her husband.

A remarkable change had come over him. He was still sitting on the bench, bent a little forward like someone whose ribs had been broken, and spitting out blood. But, his face was contorted into a strange expression between a grimace and a smile, and he showed his blood-stained teeth like a feral mongrel.

'There is nothing you can do about it,' he said.

He kept talking, incomprehensible things about the immortality of the Yogi and the inability of anyone to stop him. His speech was punctuated by frequent coughs as he spat out more blood.

Even as he spoke, I wondered if he meant what he was saying. This was a man of science, a rational man. If he was talking like this, what hope did the rest of us have? The clouds outside had become darker, and the rain had returned with a visceral ferocity.

THIRTY-TWO

At the police headquarters, Rukmini was waiting for us. She started howling inconsolably as soon as she saw Ashutosh, grabbing the front of his shirt. It was impossible to understand her words. The only thing I could make out was a name she repeated: Nandini. As I would learn very soon, this was the name of her daughter.

The ACP made her sit down and have a glass of water. This calmed her a little and she told us the reason why she had come to us: her daughter was missing.

'Since when?' demanded Ashutosh, almost leaping up from his chair.

'Yesterday,' she replied.

'Why didn't you come to us earlier?'

'I kept trying to call you all night, but no one answered the phone at your house.'

Between coughs and tears, Rukmini told us what had happened. She had returned home last afternoon from the office of Pratham Prakash to find the driver waiting for her. He usually picked up Nandini from school but had come home that day without her. He had gone to fetch her as usual, only to be informed by the school authorities that her father had already taken her away.

'Where is Dr Bose?' said Ashutosh. 'She must be with him.'

'That's impossible!' Rukmini cried. 'He is not even in town. He has gone to a conference in New Zealand.'

Ashutosh and I looked at each other. Dr Bose was missing from Calcutta yet again at a time when a dead girl had turned up.

'Do you know exactly where he is?' the ACP said. 'Do you have the number of his hotel?'

Rukmini fished out a piece of folded paper from her purse and gave it to Ashutosh. He took me aside and asked me to confirm this. While I was doing that in another room, the ACP tried to explain to Rukmini his suspicions about her husband and his possible involvement in the crimes. I was happy to not witness another round of hysteria that was sure to overwhelm her.

First, I called up Air India and Indian Airlines to check if they had a Dr Bose on any of their outbound flights over the past few days. They quickly confirmed that they did not. Then I got the operator to connect me to the international number that Rukmini had given us. As we had expected, it did not belong to any hotel or conference venue. Can you guess where it connected me? The Vasant Sena ashram in Auckland! The person who received my call mistook me to be a curious disciple and I continued to indulge her as I extracted all the information I needed. She told me that the ashram had never hosted a medical conference in the past and never intended to do so in the future. However, some new VHS tapes of Yogi Premananda's sermons were now available. Would I be interested in getting a few of these delivered to my home? I gently put the phone down and disconnected the line.

The DCP arrived at his office around 10 a.m. to find us waiting for him. The expression that came over his face communicated in no uncertain terms that he was not too happy to find us outside his office. His displeasure was probably aggravated by the gaggle of journalists who were also waiting for him. They had started gathering since the news of the dead had spread. The police department leaked information like a broken pipe.

Our boss barely acknowledged our salutes and indicated that we should follow him into his office.

'What are you doing here, Ashutosh?' he barked, without even asking us to sit. 'Why have you not gone on leave yet?'

'I did not think this was an appropriate time to go on leave sir,' the ACP replied. His voice was calm, but steely, sharp.

'What do you mean? I had given you clear orders…'

Ashutosh did not let him finish. 'I believe doing my duty is more important than following your orders,' he said.

I don't know if Ashutosh intended it, but these words managed to rattle DCP Mukherjee. He was sipping water nonchalantly from a glass and looking through some papers on his desk. On hearing Ashutosh, he put the glass down with a clatter and fixed his eyes on us.

'What the fuck are the two of you up to?' he shouted.

Ashutosh did not shout back but continued in a calm voice. 'Do you know that another dead girl has been found this morning at Princep Ghat?'

'Of course, I know, but what has that got to do with you? Both of you are off this case.'

There was no way I could have predicted what Ashutosh would do next. In a swift motion, he arched over the wide table between the DCP and us, and grabbing the senior officer by his collar, pulled him towards us. The glass of water fell to the floor and shattered. Almost spitting into DCP Mukherjee's face, Ashutosh said: 'Listen to me you motherfucker: neither you nor your Yogi can take me off this case till I have saved Rukmini's daughter and put *him* into a cage.'

He released the boss and let him fall back in his chair. The DCP was catatonic with fury, almost speechless. When he managed to regain his breath, he threatened to get us suspended, but his voice was so shaky, so devoid of conviction, that even I could not help smiling at him.

This infuriated DCP Mukherjee even more. 'I will destroy your careers,' he screamed.

'Do you know what I will do?' replied Ashutosh. 'I will walk out of this room and tell the journalists about the Yogi's new-moon ritual. I will also tell them that you are a member of Vasant Sena and that you are protecting him.'

'What nonsense is this?'

'Are you or are you not a member of Vasant Sena?'

The question seemed to take all the wind out of the DCP. He averted his eyes from us and looked away. His face had an expression I had seen many times on the faces of criminals, after they have confessed to a crime at the end of a long interrogation.

This also had a strange effect on me: I was filled with revulsion to my gut. How far had the pestilence of Yogi

Premananda's hatred and greed spread? Who else knew about this and had kept quiet, made no effort to save the innocent? The DCP's office had large windows, and yet, it seemed so claustrophobic to me. I could hear cars on Lalbazaar Street below; the voices of beggars and hawkers and pedestrians floated up to us in an indecipherable cacophony. Yet, all the sounds of the city seemed to have receded, like the waves of an ebbing sea, leaving behind on the beach the carcass of a rotting monster.

'What do you want?' said the DCP in a defeated voice.

Ashutosh had planned it all out. He was going to take three teams and launch a search and seize operation on Yogi Brahmananda Hospital. The girls trapped there needed to be saved first. The DCP would be arranging for the search and arrest warrants immediately. Our boss did not demur but only indicated his consent by a nod of his head.

Before leaving the room, the ACP turned to him and said with as much disgust as he could muster in his voice: 'The next time you are giving the Yogi a blowjob, tell him that I am coming for him. No matter how many children he kills and how many hearts he eats, the Yogi is not bulletproof. I shall shoot him like one shoots a mad dog on the streets.'

We faced some resistance at the entrance to the hospital. The private security guards tried to prevent the police from entering the premises. Their chief demanded to see our documents, the search warrant, court orders, and threatened to call the chief minister's office. His entire team was taken into custody and charged with interfering with police work. When he was being arrested, the chief, outraged by what he described to be illegal action by the police and jurisdictional overreach, tried to resist. All he had to do was abandon his post and go and sit in the van, but he would not cooperate, so the constables did the needful. One of them broke his nose with a sharp jab of the elbow; another fractured his right hand at two places. The chief lay on the road for a few minutes, moaning and cursing, till an ambulance came and took him away. The other members of his team meekly climbed into the police van waiting for them and were driven away.

Having secured the two entrances, we hurried into the campus in an assault formation, our weapons aimed in front of us. We were expecting more resistance. What? What? Oh yes, there was a huge crowd of patients at the gates when we arrived there around midday. Seeing us and sensing trouble, it melted away. We set up a perimeter at a distance of a few feet, and a larger crowd gathered beyond it. Someone had informed the press, and journalists also started turning up in ones and twos, aiming their darts of questions at us, but we had no time to engage them.

The campus was surprisingly empty, with few patients and fewer medical and non-medical staff. Our officers had instructions to round up all the employees and volunteers in front of the reception.

Ashutosh and I headed straight for the paediatrics department, along with a smaller team. It was empty; there was not a single child in the wards. Only a junior doctor and two compounders were around.

'Where are all the children?' demanded Ashutosh.

'They have all gone home,' the doctor replied. He was a lean, bespectacled young man, possibly still in his twenties. 'What is the problem?' he said.

'A girl who was here yesterday was found dead this morning. Where are all your patient records?'

The doctor did not reply but stared at us mutely. We soon discovered that all the records had been destroyed, burnt to ashes that lay in a pile on the floor of the head of the department's office. Now, it was obvious why the guards had tried to stall us. They must have been tipped-off and were trying to destroy all the records before we could get our hands on them.

Ashutosh and I ran to the psychiatry department. The nurse who was there the previous day was on duty again. She was surprised to see us but was composed enough to keep on lying and stalling. When we told her that we were there for Asima, she calmly informed us that there had never been any patient by that name in the hospital.

The ACP snatched the register from her, only to find that the page with Asima's details had been torn out. We hurried into the wards. There were a few patients, but the door to the room in which we had met Asima was shut. A lock was hanging on it.

Ashutosh took out his revolver and fired at it.

We entered it to find that the room had been completely transformed. There were no beds, nor patients. Its walls were lined with wooden cabinets, filled with glass vials of medicine. Even the walls of the room had been repainted. The day we met Asima, they had been a faded white; now it was a light yellow. Someone had cleaned the floor of the room recently, and the smell of formaldehyde hung in the air.

'Where is Dr Bose?' Ashutosh asked the nurse.

'He is not in town,' she replied, almost smiling at us. 'He has gone for a conference in New Zealand.'

'Show me his office.'

The nurse did not demur and escorted us to the office. Its doors were not locked. Everything was spick and span. The large French windows were open, the late afternoon sun streaming in. In the centre of the room was a large wooden table with a glass top. There were no papers on it, nor stationery; only a sparkling typewriter of German make. On the right of the table was a large, open cabinet with case studies neatly catalogued. Towards the left of the room was an iron bed, where patients were probably made to lay down for examination.

'Sister, we know very well that Dr Bose is not in New Zealand,' said Ashutosh. 'He has not even left town.'

'I don't know what you are talking about,' she replied.

'We don't have time…'

The ACP moved closer to the open window as something had arrested his attention. Without saying a word, he flipped out his gun, took aim and fired at something outside. He had missed his aim: we realized it, because he cursed loudly. Then, he climbed over the window and jumped out.

The nurse cried out in horror.

I ran to the window and looked down, along with the two constables who were with us. We had a clear view of the parking area. Ashutosh was already on his feet and running towards something.

With only a moment's hesitation, I followed him out of the window.

Since I was less athletic than Ashutosh, I landed on my left shoulder instead of my feet. As I got up, I felt a sharp jab of pain. I feared I might have dislocated it. The fall had also knocked my breath out, and it took me a moment to get my bearings back – just in time.

Had I been a second late, a reckless ambulance driver would have run me over. The idiot driving the vehicle swerved in the nick of time, and I somehow managed to jump out of the way.

I had taken out my gun, when Ashutosh drove up in his blue Ambassador.

'That's him, that's Dr Bose,' he shouted. 'He's got Nandini.' I jumped into the car.

The two gates of the hospital we knew about were secured by the police, but here was another one we had not known about. The ambulance headed straight for it, and finding no obstruction, drove straight out of the hospital. We were not too far behind.

The ambulance raced down Santoshpur Road. It was headed straight for the Eastern Metropolitan Bypass, the rope of a new road that girdled the eastern fringe of the city, connecting Garia to Dumdum. Civic amenities had not yet found their way down this stretch. The road was flanked by forests, punctuated by semi-rural settlements of refugees, mostly from the erstwhile East Pakistan. A fog of mystery still hung over the area. People would avoid taking the road after dark, fearing robbers; there were rumours of bodies, strangled or their heads smashed in, being found on the sides of the road.

The driver of the ambulance seemed to have no such concerns and was speeding towards the highway, barely keeping within the speed limit. The traffic on this road was sparse, but there were still enough vehicles to prevent us from engaging Dr Bose.

Ashutosh had already contacted the Gariahat and Kasba police stations as well as the control room, asking for re-enforcements. He had also instructed them to set up roadblocks all along the Bypass and given the number and description of the ambulance. We were confident that there was no way it could escape. Unknown to him, Dr Bose was rushing into a trap.

It took him no more than ten minutes to reach the highway. However, instead of turning left towards Dumdum, as I had expected, he turned right. The road did not go too far in this direction, so I was confused about where he was going.

'What the fuck is he doing?' I said.

'He is going to the Vasant Sena ashram,' said Ashutosh.

He was right. The ashram was on the southern edge of the city, beyond the jurisdiction of the city authorities. It was a sprawling compound spread over several acres, surrounded by a high, concrete wall and guarded by armed units of Vasant Sena. If Dr Bose managed to reach it, there would be no way to save Nandini.

He had also probably thought of it and accelerated his vehicle. Ashutosh too sped up, but it was becoming increasingly clear that we would not be able to chase him down.

'Take the wheel,' said the ACP, and without any warning, opened his door and leaned out of the car. Even as I managed to steady the Ambassador, he took aim and fired at the ambulance. The shots found their mark, taking out the tyres.

The vehicle swerved from left to right, veering unsteadily from side to side, before crashing into a gulmohar tree by the side of the highway.

Slowing down, I stopped our car a few metres behind it.

'Dr Bose,' cried Ashutosh, getting out of the car. 'Put your hands above your head and step out of your vehicle.'

The ACP had opened his door and was standing behind it, his revolver aimed at the crashed ambulance. As there was no response, he stepped out of his cover. No sooner had he done that than the doctor opened fire on us.

Luckily, he was a bad shot. His bullets only ricocheted off the bonnet of our car. Ashutosh took cover immediately.

'Dr Bose!' the ACP shouted again. 'There is no way you can escape. More police force is on its way.'

There was no response, so he continued: 'Your vehicle is of no use, and you must also be injured. So why don't you surrender instead of trying to get all of us killed?'

'Bastard!' Dr Bose shouted back. 'You think I don't know what's going on between you and Rukmini?'

Ashutosh looked at me for a moment. 'We can talk about it, Dr Bose,' he shouted back, 'but we don't need to behave like medieval brutes.'

The doctor emerged from the crash. His expensive suit was muddy, with a few missing buttons. He was limping slightly. His gun was pointed straight at us.

'Put your gun down,' said the ACP. 'I'm here only for your daughter.'

'I know,' the doctor replied, 'has she sent you?'

'You must let us take Nandini.'

'No.' He opened fire from his automatic but the bullets missed his mark.

Ashutosh, however, did not miss his target. The post-mortem report would reveal that two bullets from his service revolver had found their mark. One was lodged in Dr Bose's left shoulder, the other had found his heart.

The doctor's body fell like a sawed-off tree.

We heard the blaring sirens of the reinforcements arriving. Ashutosh did not wait for them but ran to the ambulance; I followed him, unsure if there were more men hiding in it.

There was no one, except Nandini. She was curled up on the passenger's seat, sleeping, probably drugged. She had slept through the turmoil.

THIRTY-THREE

The Calcutta Film Society was screening a special show of Satyajit Ray's *Ganashatru* on October 27, at their premises in Bhowanipur. As a member, Ashutosh got two invitations, and asked me to accompany him. He had a poor opinion of my cultural education and was always encouraging me to attend these events. I found them boring, mostly.

On our way to the screening, he told me that this film was an adaptation of a famous Norwegian play. I had never heard of the play or the playwright. Ashutosh must have told me, but I don't remember. The ACP was a great fan of Ray and had watched all his films. I had also watched the Apu one and *Goopy-Bagha*, which my parents took me to at Minerva.

We caught a glimpse of the filmmaker at the screening. He looked tired and unwell. When he waved at the audience, there was an uproarious round of applause that refused to die out till the organizers intervened. The compère gave a brief introduction to the film: it had already been shown at Cannes and would get a theatrical release in India early next year. Then the lights dimmed, and the show started.

Ray, his wife, and son sat in the first row. We were a few rows behind. I found that I could not concentrate on the film and my thoughts wandered elsewhere.

Things had moved at a rapid pace since the raid at the hospital. When we returned to the headquarters with Nandini, and DCP Mukherjee got the full report of the encounter, he had no option but to call a press conference. He tried to explain how we had finally cracked the case. But, it ended in utter chaos. The journalists demanded to know why they had been kept in the dark, and even worse, misled on purpose. A heated exchange began when the chief crime reporter of *The Statesman*, Gayatri Vasudevan, wanted to know if there had been an attempted cover-up because some senior officers of the department were members of the Vasant Sena.

'What do you mean?' the DCP said.

Though the reporter had not named him, Biswajit Mukherjee knew that this was an accusation. His face was an ugly shade of purple.

'Can you deny that you are a member of Vasant Sena?' Gayatri continued. 'Is that the reason the department has gone easy on Yogi Premananda, even after the riots? Is that why it took you so long to nab the killer of innocent children?'

The DCP stormed out of the meeting without answering any questions.

He spent the rest of the day trying to figure out who had leaked the information to the press. The obvious suspect was Ashutosh. But he had no opportunity to find out. He was transferred the next day to the police training college and Ashutosh was put in charge.

In the film, a doctor, played by Soumitra Chatterjee, a resident of a fictional town, diagnoses water-borne diseases among his patients and starts an investigation, leading to the discovery that the *charanamrita* (holy water) of the temple is contaminated. But, when he tries to make this knowledge public, the entire town turns against him. Some are motivated by religious fervour; others have simpler commercial motives: if people learn of the contamination of the water, the tourist inflow in the town will stop, leading to losses. When the local newspaper rescinds its offer to publish his piece on this discovery, the doctor calls a public meeting to make the people of the town aware. Before he can read his piece, however, the meeting is hijacked by his brother, who is also the chairman of the municipality. He questions the doctor's faith in religion and accuses him of slandering the temple. The meeting ends in chaos, with the citizens of the town turning against the doctor and calling him an enemy of the people. The doctor's house is attacked, his landlord asks him to vacate it, he is sacked from his job at the hospital, and even his daughter is not spared. She, too, loses her job at the school where she taught.

Though it was a Ray film, I did not find it so interesting. There was just too much dialogue. Ashutosh, however, was engrossed. Did he imagine himself in the same role as the protagonist in the film? A lone scientific warrior in conflict with the demon of superstition and blind religion? It was quite possible.

My thoughts were elsewhere. Ashutosh considered the raid at the hospital to be a complete success, but I did not quite agree with him. It was true that we had managed to rescue Nandini and reunite her with her mother, but what of the other girls we had seen the previous day at the paediatrics department? All records had been destroyed before we could seize them. Someone must have tipped off the hospital before our arrival. The police department leaks, as I have told you, like a broken pipe. Both Ashutosh and I suspected our former boss, DCP Mukherjee, but there was precious little we could prove against him.

Some questions remained unanswered, and this made me very uneasy. I had listed these in my notebook:

1. We found no consignment of human organs – leave alone the hearts of the murdered children – at the hospital. In fact, it had no facility for organ transplant, so where did the operations take place?
2. There was no trace of Viaspan or the University of Wisconsin solution at the hospital. If you remember, this solution was used to preserve human organs. According to a government report Ashutosh had found out, the hospital was its biggest importer that year. This discovery had made him suspicious. So where had the entire consignment disappeared?
3. This was even more worrying: If Dr Bose had not tried to escape, thus proving his guilt, what would we have charged him with? It is not a crime to find a father with his daughter, and he could easily make up some excuse for not being in Auckland.

When I lay in my bed at night, such thoughts prevented me from going to sleep.

Ashutosh did not seem in the least worried by all this. Soon after taking charge, he decided we must conduct a search and seize operation at Yogi Premananda's ashram. This was, as you can imagine, easier said than done. Our political bosses were communists and they had no great love for an aggressive religious movement like Vasant Sena; in fact, the Party was already in conflict with it. But giving sanction to an official enquiry was a different matter. The government could not ignore the political costs of such a move. The ACP, however, was very insistent, buzzing around Lalbazaar and the Writers' Buildings like a moral wasp, ready to sting anyone who disagreed with him.

I disagreed with him. I remembered what Tim had told me about the hapless raid at Yogi Premananda's ashram in Auckland. I did not want a repetition of that in Calcutta and tried to dissuade Ashutosh from taking a hasty call.

But my efforts were not successful; the ACP was ready to launch the operation any day and was just waiting for a green light from the government.

From the screening, we went back to Lalbazaar in Ashutosh's blue Ambassador. He was driving. Evenings had started coming early. Though it was not 6 p.m. yet, the streetlights were all on, casting a yellow pall over the roads. The ACP was very excited about the film, because he felt it validated some theory he had.

'That's what I was telling you,' he said. 'No one really cares about religion. It's always about the money.'

We stopped at a signal near the Academy of Fine Arts. This road was a little dark, close to the racecourse and the wilderness of the Maidan. Though Diwali was still a day away, you could hear the occasional fireworks; at times a rocket would explode into a million stars in the sky above us.

'I don't understand,' I said.

Ashutosh explained that in the film, the doctor's brother was not really a devout person. His only motivation was commerce.

'What is your point?' I asked.

The ACP smiled and replied: 'The same commercial motives apply to Yogi Premananda. He was a chemistry professor. Surely, he cannot believe that eating human hearts will make him immortal.'

'So why is he doing it?'

'He is not eating the hearts. He is selling them somewhere.'

This made perfect sense. What did not make sense was why the Yogi's devotees would agree to killing their daughters and offering their hearts to the guru.

'Why are you so surprised?' said Ashutosh. 'In our country, most people don't want daughters. The rate of female infanticide is so high, don't you know? In every census, we learn of the horrible sex ratio in this country.'

Ashutosh's theory was this: the Yogi had found himself an international buyer of human organs. If we were to trust Hope's testimony, it seems that he had tried to trick his devotees into killing themselves so he could sell off their organs. This had obviously not worked out as planned. After returning to India he had come up with a better plan – to get his devotees to sacrifice their children for their organs. It was simple, yet so effective. There was no fear of getting caught, as no devotee would betray him.

The signal had turned green and we were moving again. Our car merged into the heavy traffic on Chowringhee. With all the lights and noise and people, it seemed nearly impossible that such darkness, such atavism also existed among us.

At the department, two visitors were waiting for Ashutosh: Sabyasachi Khan and Afreen. The ACP was not really interested in meeting them. He did not want to be distracted from the current case. But they were very insistent. He would have directed them to another officer, but they came bearing a letter of introduction from a senior Party official. This person was a vocal critic of Vasant Sena. Perhaps Ashutosh had thought that if he helped Afreen and Sabyasachi, he would be able to curry a few favours with this Party member.

He invited them into his office; I followed them.

After the initial introduction, Ashutosh offered them tea. They politely declined, but I did not.

'How many sugars?' the ACP asked as usual.

'One, sir,' I said.

'Milk?'

'Yes, sir.'

Handing me the cup, Ashutosh made himself some tea and asked the visitors to apprise us of the details of the case.

Sabyasachi began by producing a copy of the FIR they had filed at the Park Circus police station. Ashutosh barely glanced at it and nonchalantly dropped it on the table. Sabyasachi began to tell us the sequence of events I have already told you.

When the narration ended, the ACP asked: 'What is the status of the investigation?'

'The officers at the police station don't tell us anything,' Sabyasachi replied. 'So, we have come to you.'

'Don't worry, we shall find out very soon.'

'Thank you, sir. We are very hopeful.'

Ashutosh extinguished his cigarette and picked up the postcard-sized photograph of the missing person that was lying on the table, along with the FIR.

'What did you say his name was again?' he asked.

'I'm sorry,' replied Sabyasachi, 'I don't think we…'

'Muzammil Ibrahim,' said Afreen. Her voice was calm, but it had the same effect as an exploding grenade in a packed cinema.

'What did you say?' Ashutosh sat up ramrod straight.

'Muzammil Ibrahim.'

'Where did he work?'

'At an NGO…'

'Pratham Prakash?' Ashutosh did not let her finish.

'Exactly,' said Sabyasachi, 'but how did you know?'

The ACP did not answer. He got up and started pacing the room. The visitors stared at him, puzzled.

'Something is wrong,' Ashutosh said at length.

'What do you mean?' Sabyasachi asked.

'The director of Pratham Prakash is a very good friend. Her assistant is also called Muzammil Ibrahim. But…' He stopped and lit another cigarette.

'But what?'

'This is not his picture.'

Ashutosh dialled a number from the phone on his table. There was no answer from the other end.

'Who you calling? Mrs Bose?' I asked. I was getting quite anxious as well. If this was the picture of Muzammil Ibrahim, who was the person who worked at Pratham Prakash?

'Yes,' said Ashutosh, 'something is not right.'

Thinking for a minute or two, he said: 'I think we must go over to Rukmini's house right away.'

Asking the visitors to wait in Ashutosh's office, we set out immediately.

THIRTY-FOUR

The streetlamp in front of Rukmini's house had gone kaput. It was flickering in a rhythm, alternately throwing a bucket of light on the road, then casting it into darkness. We parked the car near it, and Ashutosh turned off the ignition. He had driven for twenty minutes, covering the seven kilometres between Lalbazaar and New Alipore, without saying a word. I knew better than to verbalize the questions ricocheting in my brain.

As he was getting out of the car, I also opened my door, but he asked me not to follow him. I was not happy to let him go alone. Perhaps to reassure me and convince me to not come along, the ACP took out his revolver and removed the safety latch.

Leaving me waiting in the passenger seat of the car, he walked briskly towards the bungalow in which Rukmini lived.

From where I was, I could see that all the lights in the bungalow were off. But, on its window sills and balconies were lines of earthen lamps. Their flames flickered in the breeze, in unison, like a visual representation of a silent musical piece. Surrounded by the pitch-dark garden, the building looked like a ship out at sea.

In the garden was a cadamba tree in full bloom. The scent of its flowers wafted in the wind towards me. Did Ashutosh perceive it as he opened the wrought iron gates of the garden? Did he glance at the marble plaque outside that still bore the name of Dr Raktim Bose?

What? What? Be a little patient, will you? Haven't I told you everything already? Every time you distract me, it is such an enormous effort to recollect all my thoughts again.

So, where were we?

Yes, Ashutosh; so, he crossed the gravel path of the garden hurriedly and rang the bell beside the thick wooden doors of the building, at the same time crying out Rukmini's name.

The door opened almost immediately, and she stood in front of him, wearing a gorgeous *kanjivaram* sari and carrying a bronze plate in her left hand. The plate had flowers, sweets and a lamp, all the paraphernalia for a puja.

'I was wondering when you would come,' she said.

'Why did you not take my calls?' he demanded.

She did not answer. Instead, seeing the gun in his hand, Rukmini threw her head back and laughed. 'Must you always come to my house with your muzzle unsheathed and smoking?' she said, before putting her mouth on his and invading the barricade of his teeth with her tongue.

When she was done, she held his hand and took him into the house. In the process, she grabbed his service revolver and disarmed him.

The drawing room was completely dark. As Rukmini turned on all the lights, the first thing Ashutosh saw was the shrine dedicated to Yogi Premananda. It was exactly as he had seen it the last time. The only difference was that someone had put a garland of fresh marigold around it. Two new incense sticks were burning in front of it.

Ashutosh (*almost shouting*): What the fuck is that?

Rukmini (*startled*): Why are you shouting?

Ashutosh (*still in a loud voice*): Why is that shrine still here? Why haven't you thrown it out?

Rukmini: Why would I do that? He is my guru.

Ashutosh (*surprised*): Guru? After all that he has done? Even after he tried to kill your daughter?

Rukmini: I would happily kill my father, my mother, my brother, my husband, and even my daughter, if the guru asked for it.

Ashutosh stares at her, bewildered. Rukmini starts walking away from him.

Ashutosh: What?

Rukmini: If the guru asked me, I would kill my daughter, cut out my heart and present it to him on this plate.

Ashutosh: What nonsense is this? Where is Nandini?

Rukmini: Don't worry about it. She is upstairs, sleeping. It's not new moon tonight; that's tomorrow.

Ashutosh: What are you talking about?

Ashutosh starts to move towards Rukmini, but she turns around sharply, pointing the gun at him.

Rukmini: Don't even think about it

Ashutosh: Rukmini, this is not a joke. The gun is loaded. Give it back.

Rukmini: Do I look like I am joking?

He takes another step. She fires. It's not a wayward shot. The bullet lodges in his shoulder. He staggers backward and falls.

Sitting in the car, I may have heard the shot, or it may have been camouflaged by the sound of fireworks emanating from buildings in the area. A couple of minutes earlier, I had seen a light come on in Rukmini's house, possibly in her drawing room. The light made me relax a little. It probably meant that things were fine.

I got out of the car, and closing the door, stood leaning against it. There was a cigarette in my hand, but I had forgotten to light it. Ashutosh would be back any moment, I thought, with some information on Muzammil Ibrahim. Well, that was not his original name – at least this much was now clear. We also knew that he had already quit his job at Pratham Prakash. But where did he go after that? And, why had he taken on a false identity in the first place? Perhaps, Rukmini would have an address, maybe even a photograph of this man that we could then show Afreen. If this man had taken her husband's identity, it was more than likely that she knew him.

Even as I was thinking of all this, I felt a furry body brush up against my legs. I looked down and found a mongrel. It looked bony and had sharp pointed ears, like that of a fox. I did not see it coming. Now, it was rubbing its back against my legs. Though I did not dislike dogs, I did not like them very much either. This one had fleas in its patchy fur. Feeling rather irritated, I kicked it. The dog retreated, yelping in pain. The kick was not too hard, so it was not hurt. Its cries were complaints against my betrayal. I felt guilty immediately. The dog limped away into the darkness.

As Ashutosh sat on the sofa, holding a towel to his shoulder, Rukmini began telling him a most fantastic narrative.

'Raktim and I tried for three years to get pregnant, but we did not succeed,' she said. 'Then, on the advice of his parents, we sought the help of the Yogi. The first time I saw him was at his ashram. It was love at first sight. I had never seen any man like him. On hearing about our problem, he asked me to volunteer at the ashram and get more involved with the work of Pratham Prakash.'

A month later, she was pregnant. When Nandini was born, Rukmini took her to the Yogi. 'When the time comes,' the Yogi told her, 'you will cut out her heart and give it to me.'

Perhaps, it was the loss of blood, thought Ashutosh, because none of this was making any sense to him. She spoke in a soft sing-song voice that made him even more soporific. The blood from the wound had drenched the left side of his shirt and was now staining the sofa and the red carpet at his feet.

The ACP was not worried. He knew that sooner or later, I would come looking for him. In the meanwhile, he wanted to ask a few things:

Ashutosh: So why did you come to me when Dr Bose kidnapped Nandini?

Rukmini: He didn't kidnap Nandini.

Ashutosh: What do you mean? We chased him down and rescued her.

Rukmini: You are such a bulldog. He ran so you ran after him.

Ashutosh: But he was in the hospital with Nandini when he was supposed to be in Auckland.

Rukmini: He was never supposed to be in Auckland.

Ashutosh: You told me…

Rukmini: Exactly. *I told you*. I told you that he was in Auckland. I gave you the list of dates when he was supposedly travelling out of Calcutta, corresponding to the list of dates when the bodies of the dead girls were found. I even had to tell you about Kumkum Kumari.

Ashutosh: So, he was innocent.

Rukmini: No one is innocent.

Ashutosh: I killed him. You made me kill him.

Rukmini: Don't be so outraged. Remember when I had snatched the gun from you the first time, and how you had bragged about killing more than one person with it?

Ashutosh: What was the point of all this, Rukmini?

Rukmini: You see, my husband might have been infertile, but he was not stupid. When Kumkum was sacrificed, he started suspecting me and others of the Vasant Sena. So, I went to the police, to you.

Ashutosh: And when he saw me at the hospital…

Rukmini: He did not think of you as a police officer trying to rescue Nandini. He saw his wife's lover. He was trying to protect Nandini. How would he know that you were not with the Vasant Sena?

Ashutosh: Your plan worked out perfectly. But, that still leaves one question unanswered.

Rukmini: What?

Ashutosh: If Dr Bose was not involved, who was performing the surgeries?

Rukmini: You have already met him. Look behind you.

The ACP turned around and saw Dr Sushovan Sengupta standing near the entrance to the room. He was smiling.

'Good evening officer,' he said, 'can I check your wound?'

Feeling rather guilty about kicking the dog, I decided to smoke the cigarette I had been fiddling with for so long. There was no matchbox or lighter on me, so I decided to look in the car. The flaps on the doors were empty. I pulled open the glove compartment on the dashboard. There was nothing in there either to light my cigarette, but something else spilled out: a large brown envelope folded in half.

I picked it up to get a better view in the flickering streetlamp and recognized it immediately. This was the envelope Tim Taylor had sent me with the photographs taken on the day of the Vasant Sena rally. Distracted by the investigation, we had forgotten all about it.

Now, I took out the photographs again and started looking at them very carefully. I had only glanced through them hurriedly. Then, as now, these seemed the most detailed documentation of that fateful day. No such photograph had been published in any newspaper, nor were there any in police records. I thought we should add these to our files. These clearly showed the extent to which Vasant Sena had armed itself. Its members could be seen carrying sophisticated, automatic weapons, imported from western manufacturers. Even the police department did not have such weapons. Perhaps, if we showed these photographs to the Party leaders, Ashutosh would get the green light to conduct the raid on the ashram.

Then, in the flickering light of the streetlamp, I saw what we should have spotted long back. In one of the pictures, at the corner of the frame, stood Muzammil Ibrahim, in full Vasant Sena costume.

No, no, you are right. It was not Muzammil. It was the man who had introduced himself to us by that name. Nor was he a Muslim, for why would a Muslim man wear the Vasant Sena uniform and join their rally?

I decided that Ashutosh needed to see this immediately. Why was he taking so much time anyway? Putting the photograph in my pocket, I hurried towards Rukmini's house.

THIRTY-FIVE

All the lamps in Rukmini's house were extinguished and it was shrouded in a forbidding darkness. The hinges on the wrought iron gates needed to be oiled. If I had to push them open, it would have warned the inmates of the house. Luckily for me, Ashutosh had left just enough of a gap for me to slip through. The gravel path in the garden was slippery with moss. Fearing that I would lose my balance and fall, I was compelled to tread carefully. For some reason, I decided not to go and ring the bell on the front door. Instead, I approached the house with stealth, concealing myself in the shadow of the trees. My service revolver was out in my hand.

What had made me wary? It's difficult to tell really. Call it the intuition of a policeman. My memories of that evening are a little muddled, and it is impossible to analyze them. Now that you ask me, I think, what might have triggered this uneasy feeling was that I could see no light anywhere in the building except the drawing room. I must have also seen the shadows then: the illuminated window of the drawing room revealed not two – as I had expected – but three human silhouettes. They were moving very, very slowly. Though I was quite sure that being in light, they would never be able to see me, I kept low as I approached the window.

As I looked in, I saw a strange scene unfolding. The ACP was sitting on a chair, with his back to me. Dr Sushovan Sengupta (What the fuck is he doing here, I thought) was sitting facing him, on a low stool. Dr Sengupta was talking:

'The Yogi is the only truth. Everything else is maya.'

Ashutosh laughed. 'You think this hocus-pocus gives you the licence to take the lives of innocent children?'

'When the Yogi becomes immortal…' began Rukmini, but Ashutosh cut her off.

'No one becomes immortal by eating someone's else heart,' he said. 'This is all illusion, magic. Even a street performer can do this stuff.'

'Nonsense!' shouted Dr Sengupta. 'How can you compare the Yogi to a street magician?'

'He is worse, actually,' replied Ashutosh. 'Street performers don't kill children.'

'You don't know anything,' said Rukmini, calmly. 'When the power of the Yogi is revealed to you…'

The ACP cut her off again. 'Let me tell you what is going to happen. When I do not return to the headquarters, the entire police force will descend on this place. If you surrender, you will live. Then you might get to entertain a judge with your stories. But, with all my experience, I can tell you, the judge will not be very amused, and is more than likely to hand you a capital sentence.'

'We will never surrender,' Dr Sengupta said.

The ACP laughed again. 'Then you will be shot dead like a dog in the street,' he said. Though he was wounded and disarmed, Ashutosh could make such grandiloquent statements and find everything amusing because he knew that sooner or later, I would get suspicious and turn up to save him.

'Let me give you some advice,' he continued. 'Why don't you untie me and let me arrest you? We don't need to go into the trouble of an encounter, and blood and gore. I'll simply call the department and we'll take you in. The back-up team will be here any moment.'

'Then, we don't have a moment to lose, do we?'

The last words were uttered by none of the three people in the room. The voice was familiar, and looking in its direction, I found the source as well: Muzammil Ibrahim.

'Ah, Mr Ibrahim,' said Ashutosh, 'you are the one I was looking for.'

'Don't call me by that filthy Muslim name,' the newcomer cried out.

'So, what should I call you then? Bhajan Kaul? Is that your real name?'

Ashutosh's interlocutor seemed a little taken aback. He had probably not expected that his identity would be revealed so easily. 'What have you done with the real Muzammil Ibrahim?' the ACP continued.

'How does it matter? Maybe he is buried somewhere, maybe the fish in the Hooghly have eaten him.'

'His wife and landlord are waiting in the police headquarters at this moment. I have to take back some information.'

'Let us just be very clear about one thing officer,' said Bhajan. 'You are not going anywhere.'

As he stepped into the light, I saw that he was wearing the Vasant Sena uniform. In his hand was a large scimitar. He moved quickly to stand in front of Ashutosh. Even now, the ACP betrayed no sign of being intimidated. He still wore the familiar careless smile of defiance.

'Till now, this story has been written by me, and I shall finish it as well,' said Bhajan. 'Let me tell you what's going to happen. At the ritual tomorrow, we shall sacrifice Nandini and present her heart to the Yogi. He will consume it and become immortal. There will be no power on this earth, or in heaven or hell to stop him. But Nandini's heart is not the only one we shall give him. We shall also present your heart to him. Consider yourself lucky officer that you have been chosen for this.'

As he spoke, Bhajan had raised the scimitar to bring it down in a curve and remove Ashutosh's head from his shoulder. I was done watching passively from outside the window. Standing up, I aimed my revolver and opened fire. The scimitar fell from his hand and landed on the floor with a loud clang.

Almost immediately, Dr Sengupta returned my fire. He also took out the lights in the room, plunging it into complete darkness. Remember what I had told you about gunfights in movies? The ones in real life are nothing like that. I climbed through the window into the dark room and tried to crawl toward where I imagined Ashutosh would be. My progress was, as you can imagine, very slow, as I kept bumping into furniture. I did not dare to stand up, for fear of revealing my position. An occasional firework lit up the room. In the red and green light of one, I saw the chair in which Ashutosh was sitting had fallen over, but the ACP was no longer tied to it. This provided me with a little relief, because it meant that he was still alive.

In the light of the next rocket illuminating the skies outside, I spotted Dr Sengupta. He was standing with his back to me, a little disoriented, hunched like a cat ready to pounce. I took aim and fired. His body collapsed on the floor.

I had not even brought down my gun, when I felt a sharp stab in my back. Turning around slowly, I saw it was Rukmini. She was staring at me with bloodshot eyes, a knife in her hand. Thankfully, the knife was not big enough to cause any great damage. I know that now. Then, however, the pain was overwhelming, and I fell on my knees. Rukmini raised the knife to stab me again.

But, she did not have the opportunity. The scimitar swung across the air, cutting her head cleanly off her shoulders. The head rolled off along the floor and went under the sofa. The headless body stood for a minute or two, spewing blood in a fountain all over the place, before falling.

It was Ashutosh who had used the weapon. He, too, fell to the floor.

I crawled over to him. He was severely injured: in the crossfire, he had taken a few bullets to the body, and had managed the last act of bravado with an enormous rush of adrenaline. He did not say anything to me but closed his eyes and kept breathing heavily.

Somehow managing to find the telephone, I called police headquarters.

THIRTY-SIX

At the hospital, Ashutosh was declared 'brought dead'. He had lost a lot of blood in Rukmini's house, and he had bled out in the ambulance. A couple of days later, after the post-mortem and enquiry were completed, he was given the funeral of a martyr, with a gun salute. The body was cremated at Kalighat. I was still at the hospital then, but I got permission from the doctors to visit the crematorium for the final rites.

The ACP did not have many friends or relatives, so most of the people who turned up were from the police department. The only exceptions were Ashutosh's ex-wife, Sunita, her husband and stepson. They were standing behind everyone else, a little hesitant, unsure if their presence was acceptable or not. She was pregnant.

After the rituals, the body was rolled into the electric incinerator, and the constables started raising slogans about how Ashutosh would always remain immortal for them. Slowly, their enthusiasm waned, and they started walking away in ones and twos. I remained standing and I intended to be there till the end, though I knew the cremation would take a couple of hours. My health was not good and the medicines had made me rather disoriented. But I could not make myself go away.

Then I saw DCP Biswajit Mukherjee standing outside the building that housed the incinerators and talking to another senior officer. I walked up to him and saluted him. It was a sloppy salute, but that was the best I could do in my state. A smile broke across his sullen face, but it was a reluctant one and it did not reach his eyes.

'How are you?' he asked. His voice was infused with an inordinate amount of lightness.

'I'm good, sir.'

'You are a hero,' he said. 'So was Ashutosh.'

'Thank you, sir.'

'I'm going to recommend you for a presidential medal, both you and Ashutosh.'

'Thank you, sir,' I said, 'but we need to continue with the investigation.'

The smile on the DCP's face faltered. 'What do you mean?' he said.

'Yogi Premananda…'

'Pradip,' he did not let me complete. 'The investigation has been closed. I don't think you are aware of what happened while you were in the hospital.'

'Sir?'

'The investigation was completed, and it was found that the Yogi had nothing to do with the crimes. It was that woman, the doctor, and the Kashmiri pandit.'

'But what about the Yogi?'

DCP Mukherjee's mouth hardened into the old, familiar grimace. 'What about him?' he said.

My voice came out louder than I had intended it to: 'He was the one conducting the rituals, he was the one killing…'

'Stop it!' The DCP's voice was as cold as a metal rod. 'Listen to what I am telling you. The Yogi had nothing to do with the kidnapping and the murder of the young girls. It was Rukmini Bose, Dr Sushovan Sengupta, and Bhajan Kaul. They were the gang of illegal traders.'

The smile reappeared on his face like a watery sun on a cloudy day.

'Ashutosh and you did a very good job,' he continued. 'As I told you, I am nominating both of you for the presidential medal.'

'But we have the confessions!' I said.

'What confessions?'

'Of the parents of the girl whose body was found in the Hooghly.'

'Where is this confession? Did you get it written down? Is there a transcript? Did they sign the confession? Was there a witness?'

'I was the witness!' Yet again, my voice was louder than it should have been. 'I have seen everything, I know everything.'

The DCP waited before answering. When he spoke, it was in a deliberate staccato: 'Who is going to believe you?'

I did not understand what he meant.

'Have you seen your medical reports?' he said. 'Do you know about your condition?'

This seemed like a strange question. I had been admitted to the hospital for the injuries I had suffered at Rukmini's house.

'If you had read your own medical reports,' said the DCP, 'you would have known that your testimony would be worth nothing in court. You have been diagnosed with acute paranoia. All these things you have been telling me – some cannibalistic ritual, parent sacrificing their daughters – who will believe you? They are probably a part of your hallucinations.'

Walking up to me, the DCP put a hand on my shoulder and spoke in a voice that was almost kind: 'Get back to the hospital. You are in no state to walk around like this. When you feel better, come and see me. We will find you a nice and comfortable desk job.'

'Don't do anything stupid,' he added, before leaving.

The bus stop was half a kilometre from the crematorium. The mid-afternoon sun was beating down on the road, and after walking barely a few minutes, my shirt was drenched in sweat. A kirtan singer had started following me and performing devotional songs, possibly with the hope of getting some money from me. I had only about five rupees in my wallet and I was wondering how to tell him to go away when a Fiat Padmini drew up beside me and stopped.

The driver rolled down the window and a familiar face smiled at me: Gayatri Vasudevan, the crime reporter of *The Statesman*. 'Hello officer,' she said as brightly as the afternoon, taking off the sunglasses she was wearing.

'Hello,' I said.

'Can I drop you somewhere?'

'No, no, I am only walking to the bus stop.'

'Let me drop you there.'

I was still hesitating, but she continued, 'It's not good for you to walk around in this heat. My car has an AC.'

This was a persuasive argument and I got into the car. My sudden departure might have seemed strange to the kirtan singer. Gayatri did not stop the car at the bus stop but kept driving.

'Where are we going?' I said.

'Tell me where you live, and I will drop you there.'

'Why don't you drop me at the next bus stop?'

'Why don't we go and get a coffee first? I know a nice café.'

'I hate cafés. They always have too many people listening to everything you are saying.'

'Isn't that everywhere?' she said. 'I heard what you were talking about with DCP Mukherjee.'

'You were eavesdropping?'

'I am a reporter,' she replied. 'It's my job to find out information.'

The car had stopped at a traffic signal. Gayatri was smoking but had not rolled down the window; smoke was slowly filling up the inside of the airconditioned vehicle.

'What do you want from me?' I asked.

'I want you to tell me everything you know about the case.'

'Why?'

'The investigation has to continue.'

'You heard what the DCP said. The investigation is over.'

'Yes, the police has decided to end the investigation. But I want to continue with it.'

'Why?'

Gayatri looked at me through the smoke in the car. 'Eleven girls were killed in our city last year,' she said. 'Their hearts were cut out and their bodies thrown all over the streets. Now, barely a month after the last murder, everyone seems to have forgotten about it. No one cares that the perpetrators of the crime were not brought to justice.'

'But they were,' I protested. 'The gang of organ traders perished in a shootout with the police.'

'Yes, that's the official version. But that isn't the complete truth, is it? Yogi Premananda…'

I raised my hand to stop her. 'You heard what the DCP said: The Yogi was not involved.'

Gayatri made an impatient noise with her tongue. 'Of course, he said that. He is a member of Vasant Sena. What do you expect from him?'

'What do you want from me?'

'I want to know everything you know about the case. Weren't you telling the DCP that you are a witness to everything that happened?'

'But why me?'

'You are the one who started all of this. It was your report that first found the link between the murdered girls.'

Gayatri rolled down the window to let the accumulated smoke escape from the car. 'At present, people do not know the truth. They only know what has been told to them. We will tell them the truth.'

Since I did not say anything, she continued: 'There is a pestilence rising among us. Many see a profit in this dangerous ritual. Yogi Premananda is one of them, but he is not alone. The police brass is with him, rich businessmen, and many corrupt ones in the state machinery. So, he seems powerful, unstoppable.'

She threw out the cigarette and continued: 'But all is not lost. There is a battle ahead. The Yogi needs to be brought to justice. You and I, and people like us who can think rationally and see right through this smoke of violence, we shall stand up to the Yogi and his army. This needs to end.'

Gayatri had said all this with a serious face. Now, she looked at me and smiled. 'Tell me, are you with me in this?' she said.

There was no hesitation in my reply: 'Yes, I am.'

The signal had turned green and we were on our way again. The bright afternoon had turned into a cloudy dusk. A strong wind was picking up leaves and garbage from the streets and swirling them around. A flash of lighting cut across the sky as we drove past Jatin Das Park towards the centre of the city. A storm was coming.

ACKNOWLEDGEMENTS

As research for this novel, I read several books and watched films. Here is a short list: *Calcutta – The Living City, Vol. II: The Present and the Future* (2000) edited by Sukanta Chaudhuri, *Show Your Tongue* (1989) by Günter Grass, *Karma Cola* (1990) by Geeta Mehta, *Memoirs of Roads: Calcutta from Colonial Urbanization to Global Modernization* (2016) by Sumanta Banerjee, *Margins of Citizenship: Muslim Experiences in Urban India* (2017) by Anasua Chatterjee, and *Goyendapeeth Lalbazaar: Ek Dozen Khuner Ruddhashash Nepathakotha* (2018) by Supratim Sarkar.

ACP Ashutosh's Theory of Two Motives is inspired by Albert Camus's philosophy of murders in *The Rebel* (1992).

I watched the Calcutta trilogies of Satyajit Ray, Ritwik Ghatak, and Mrinal Sen, as well as Ray's late film *Ganashatru* (1990), and the Netflix documentary *Wild, Wild Country* (2018).

*

The idea for this novel has been with me for several years, but I began writing it only after I was commissioned by Trisha Bora to write a crime novel set in Calcutta.

The first draft of the novel was completed in the weeks following the death of my father, Somnath Das Gupta, in late-April 2017, so I have dedicated it to him.

My friend Madhavi Bhargava encouraged me to work more on it, and also introduced me to my wonderful agent Kanishka Gupta, who felt that the few chapters he read initially could actually be a novel.

Maaz Bin Bilal read several drafts and commented on it. Meghna Nag Chowdhuri helped me in many different ways while I wrote this book.

Veena Mani and Kakoli Chakraborty typed up different chapters, editing them in the process. My friends in Delhi, Suchismita Chattopadhyay, Divya Kanan, Aditya Verma, Kamalika Ghosh, Amrita Das, Darpan Singh, Aditya Remy Shah, Agne Majauskaite and Priyanka Sarkar, opened up their homes to me.

My editor, Prasun Chatterjee, along with everyone else at Pan Macmillan India, converted the manuscript into a book. Many thanks to them. Also, my thanks to Aparajita Basu for copy-editing the manuscript.

My colleagues at *Business Standard*, especially our editor Shyamal Majumdar, have always encouraged all my projects and endeavours, even if they are not journalistic.

Sumana Roy and Madhulika Liddle for the wonderful endorsements and very helpful feedback.

My mother and my sister endured the writer in the attic for all these years. Looks like there are a few more to come.